DEATH COMES FOR THE DECONSTRUCTIONIST

DEATH COMES FOR THE
DECONSTRUCTIONIST

a novel

BY
Daniel Taylor

SLANT

DEATH COMES FOR THE DECONSTRUCTIONIST

SLANT
An Imprint of Wipf and Stock Publishers
199 W. 8th Ave., Suite 3
Eugene, OR 97401

www.wipfandstock.com

ISBN 13: 978-1-62564-931-7

Cataloging-in-Publication data:

Daniel Taylor.

Death comes for the deconstructionist / Daniel Taylor.

vi + 200 p.; 23 cm

ISBN 978-1-62564-931-7

1. Murder--Investigation--Fiction. 2. Mystery fiction. 3. St. Paul (Minn.)--Fiction. I. Title.

PS3570.A92727 D3 2014

Manufactured in the USA.

"My name is Legion, for we are many."
—R. BARTHES, AFTER ST. MARK

"I do suck most wondrous philosophies from thee!
Some unknown conduits from the unknown
worlds must empty into thee!"
—AHAB TO PIP

"Where the wolves are killed off,
the foxes increase."
—FOLK SAYING

ONE

Something is wrong.

I'm not well. The voices are back.

I apologize. That's a bleak way to start. And too confessional. The world doesn't need another Underground Man or daddy-killing poet. Everyone these days is confessing everything, which leaves no space for genuinely confessing anything. Confession requires a standard, an agreed-upon line that has been crossed. It requires "ought" and "I'm sorry" and "Forgive me" and "I will not do that again." Not for us. We confess and absolve ourselves in the same breath. "I did it. I wouldn't change anything. It's who I am." To quote that great mariner-philosopher Popeye, "I yam what I yam." Self-absolving confession. How efficient. Cuts out the middleman.

Of course I'm referring to someone you've likely never heard of— Popeye. A cartoon character from the 1930s and beyond. How can I make myself understood, for God's sake, to people who don't share the same shards of pop culture that I have shored against my ruins? (Name the poet just alluded to. It's an easy one.)

Here I go again. I have to calm myself. My mind starts rolling downhill and it gathers neither moss nor meaning (Rolling Stones). Faster and faster ("Like a complete unknown / Like a rolling stone"). It's not six degrees of separation for me, it's no degrees (Sly and the Family Stone). Everything is connected—directly and remorselessly—to everything else. At the same time, nothing is connected to anything. Monism (all is one) hooks up with solipsism (one is all), and I am their bastard child.

And you have no idea what I'm talking about. And neither do I. But I do not apologize. After all, "I yam what I yam."

And the "I yam" that I am playing at the moment is detective. It's what Mrs. Pratt thinks of me, so it is what, for a time, I will be. Her husband is dead, found on the street below his thirteenth floor hotel room, a hole in his chest and a pool of blood spread nimbus-like around his head.

I like that—"nimbus-like." It just came to me this very moment. One of those synapse-leaping connections. A nimbus is a stylized halo in medieval art—which is the first thing I thought of—but also a kind of cloud, and an encryption algorithm and a Danish motorcycle and more than one literary magazine and, of course, a flying broom. And if he were alive, Dr. Pratt could make connections among all these things. Because that was his gift—making connections between things no one else would ever think to connect. And it left your head spinning.

I know because I was once a student of Dr. Pratt's. He was, for a time, a kind of intellectual saint to me—nimbus and all. And he certainly left *my* head spinning.

Dr. Pratt has been dead since spring, almost six months now, and his wife has just called me. I tell her, indirectly as usual, that she is wasting her time. I'm not a cop, or a criminal investigator, or any kind of detective. (The only thing I'm good at detecting are my own deficiencies, at which I am a master—a talent I share with my soon-to-be ex-wife.)

I'm actually nothing official, almost officially nothing. You might say I'm a researcher, with an emphasis on searcher. I search. I look into things. I don't probe people—or even events. I collect information. And then I try to make something out of it—a kind of artist of found data, you might say (think Duchamp and urinals). I try to burrow new tunnels through old hordes of information. I marry scattered facts to see if I can turn data into knowledge. (I had once hoped to turn knowledge into wisdom, but Dr. Pratt cured me of that.)

I've been a searcher all my life, but I started getting paid for it by this lawyer I know. He needed someone to interrogate the Tet Offensive in order to establish a post-traumatic shock defense for Vietnam vets. I was out of work and knew how to use a library. Since then I've become an expert on Legionnaires' disease, universal joints (General Motors and Toyota, not Ford), tempered glass, emotional stress in flight controllers and junior high social studies teachers, recidivism rates for women car thieves, bite rates for Chows, flow rates for dams, and insurance rates for epileptics. And expert on a thousand other things I wish I didn't know. My mind is clogged with a million bits of information, not one byte of which gives me a good reason to get up in the morning.

My job is not the kind that shows up on those career tests they give you. I took one in high school and they told me I was suited to be a forest ranger. The possibility had never entered my mind, but it was kind of nice knowing there was a niche for me somewhere, if I ever really needed it. You know, say I was fifty and things weren't going real well. I could maybe show up at a fire lookout tower in some forest somewhere and sort of casually bring up this test I took thirty years back and just see if I hit it off with the rangers like the test said I would. To tell the truth, I've found myself thinking of the woods lately. Lovely woods, dark and deep.

Anyway, I've been working for lawyers off and on, and Dr. Pratt's widow somehow finds out about it. I'd gotten to know her a little when I was a graduate student. You see, Pratt was my advisor as well as my professor. And guru and model and, you could say, nemesis. Mrs. Pratt was young then—thirty-something. I liked her. Okay, maybe I even had a crush on her. She was good-looking and friendly, two things you didn't see a lot among faculty wives. Most of them seemed kind of worn and faintly bitter. Too many years living with men whose first love is books.

Anyway, the phone rings, and it's Mrs. Pratt. I know of course about Dr. Pratt's murder. In fact, I had heard him speak downtown at the Midwest Modern Language Association convention only a few hours before he was killed. I went to hear him for old times' sake. I had even planned to look him up afterward to see if he remembered me. To tell the truth, I'd been a little nervous about it.

When I tell Mrs. Pratt on the phone that I had heard her husband's talk that night, she seems disconcerted. Says it's eerie—that's her word—eerie that I heard him speak just before he died. It doesn't seem eerie to me—hundreds of people heard him speak just before he died. Dying after speaking isn't any stranger than dying after eating or dying after washing the car. It always comes after something, you know what I mean?

I tell Mrs. Pratt that I'm not a private investigator or anything like one, that I am extremely unlikely to solve the crime, and that the police will only see me as a nuisance. But she insists I "look it over." She says she doesn't expect me to find the killer. She just wants more information.

"I just feel like there's something there to be seen that the police wouldn't recognize if they tripped over it. I think you can help."

It's a new concept for me. To be thought capable of helping, by a woman no less. I let the idea roll around in my psyche for a moment. I'm sure it's the main reason I say I'll think about it, even though the ache in my stomach makes me immediately wish I hadn't.

TWO

I don't decide right away. I should talk to Judy first. We haven't been back together long, and I don't want to mess things up. I have a long history of making seemingly innocent decisions that end up deflecting the universe. Zillah (my soon-to-be ex) calls it a gift for the cosmic screw-up. Big Bang-sized disasters that create galaxies of pain and black holes of confusion. It's true that I have a kind of congenital clumsiness about life that I can't seem to shake. Zillah found it moderately charming when we were dating, but it was a different story when she moved in with it.

Anyway, I decide to talk to Judy. We live together now on a rented houseboat in the Mississippi, in the shadow of the Wabasha Bridge in downtown St. Paul. Kind of an oxymoronic place—out on the river, like Huck and Jim, but going nowhere, towered over by government and office buildings on the far bank. Illusory freedom. It's not a big old tub, as houseboats go. Two tiny bedrooms up top over a fair-sized living room and galley kitchen below. Engineless, like me, neither houseboat nor occupant seaworthy.

Judy sits across the small galley table slowly chewing a hot dog on a fork that she holds up close to her face. She takes a bite and then stares at the end of the hot dog while she chews, slowly but inexorably, balanced between the pleasure of the hot dog in her mouth and the anticipation of the next bite to come. A perfect illustration of the now and not yet—the once and future hot dog.

Actually, Judy does everything slowly. Sometimes it's maddening, like being stuck in traffic behind a Grandma Moses in a Studebaker when your whole life depends on you being somewhere else. But I've decided Judy's slowness gives her a kind of dignity, like the massive stillness of a glacier. She is protracted, as God is, grinding slowly but exceedingly fine.

Now I know when I say "back together," you're thinking "girlfriend." You can't help it. We've been trained. But think sister instead. If you never thought "girlfriend," I apologize.

Yes, Judy is my sister. She is a short woman, using up most but not all of five feet. Leans toward stocky. Her hair hangs very straight and thin from the top of her head, as though placed on the crown like pick-up sticks and allowed to fall equally in each direction. She has almond-shaped eyes with sleepy, bulging lids.

Judy takes a certain pride in her shortness. "Good things come in small packages," she says with a smile.

Only Judy doesn't say it the way you or I would. She speaks very slowly. Painfully slow I would have said at one time, glacially slow. Now I prefer to think she speaks carefully, with a stateliness won of hard labor.

She doesn't actually say individual words slowly, except when she stutters. It's that she pauses between words, her eyes rolling up into her lids, trying various doors in the dim hallways of her brain, searching patiently for a word or phrase that might befriend the one already in the air. It is important to her that words, like companions, get along.

Judy's speech patterns mirror the discoveries of quantum physics. The words do not roll smoothly off her tongue in a steady progression. Rather, they leap from her lips in interrupted bursts: "Good things ... I should say, good things come ... in in ... in small packages." She often finishes in a delighted rush, much as someone crossing a stream on a narrow log hurries the last few steps and jumps to shore in relief and triumph. Then she smiles, pleased with herself and how well things turned out.

And she repeatedly inserts the phrase "I should say" into her sentences, a product of decades of correction and efforts to please. It gives her time to line up her words in a row and affords them a faintly aristocratic air. Judy has a high sense of propriety—what one *should* say or *ought* to do. It was drummed into her by our parents and by the nuns at the home. They all lived in the old world of right and wrong, and they passed it on to Judy. If you didn't know what the rules were, how were you going to know if you were doing okay?

"Well, Jude. This woman called and wants me to do some work for her."

"That's nice."

"We could use the money."

"Yes, we … we could use the money. That's for sure."

"But it would mean you'd have to be by yourself sometimes. More than now."

"Oh?"

"Well, I would have to be driving around a lot."

"I like … driving around."

"And I'd have to talk to a lot of people."

"I … I should say … I like talk … talking to people, Jon."

I chew on that.

"Of course you do. Well, why not? You wouldn't have to stay here. You could come along, at least most of the time."

Judy rosebuds her lips, raises her eyebrows, and smiles. "I could be … I should say … your sidekick."

"Sure, my sidekick."

"Like … like the Lone Ranger and … and Tonto."

"Like Pancho and Cisco."

"Like … like, I should say, like Mr. Huntley and Mr. Brinkley."

David Brinkley was Judy's first love. He gave the network news every night from Washington, while Huntley reported from New York—the only two American cities of consequence to the media at the time. Judy was a Brinkley fan. "I like his pointy nose," she used to say. "He's cute." When I was nine, I wrote a letter to Brinkley asking him to skip his signature "Goodnight, Chet" some evening and say instead, "Goodnight, Judy." It would have delighted her to no end. If he ever did, we missed it.

THREE

The next morning I call Mrs. Pratt. She invites me to her place to talk and I tell her, with a minimum of explanation, that Judy will be coming with me. Her home is on Summit Avenue in the original upscale area of St. Paul. In the nineteenth century, not long after the citizens had been sharp enough to change the name of their capital from Pig's Eye, the quality started building along and back from the bluffs overlooking the town and the Mississippi River. Dr. Pratt had taken a lot of pleasure living there, only a few blocks away and a couple of levels up the scale from where Scott Fitzgerald once lived.

I remember reading *The Great Gatsby* in one of Pratt's classes. He spoke at length about unreliable narrators, centers of consciousness, and the like. Said we couldn't trust Nick's telling of the story because Nick was *in* the story, and we couldn't trust Fitzgerald because he *wasn't* in the story, and we couldn't trust what the critics said *about* the story because they were a bundle of cultural prejudices, and we couldn't trust *him* because he wasn't us, and, most obvious of all, we couldn't trust *ourselves* because … well, I don't remember why we couldn't trust ourselves, but Dr. Pratt was very adamant about that point.

Anyway, the inside of the house, which I remember from my grad student days, is exactly what you'd expect from a man like Dr. Pratt—cosmopolitan, refined, subtle, and tasteful as hell. Everything possible has been done to minimize the rectangularity of the rooms. Screens or potted trees blunt the corners. Paintings hang just above or below where you expect, sometimes stacked three high on the wall. Most are aggressively non-representational—a slash of color here, a formal conundrum there. Nary a picture of dogs playing cards in sight.

In the living room the mostly white sofas and chairs announce in precise tones, "Admire me—do not sit." There is an undertone of metal—gleaming, reflective, polished—but the room is warmed by rich, dark cherry, floor-to-ceiling bookcases. Many of the books are beautifully bound, each in its appointed place, waiting to be opened. Just as Dr. Pratt's students waited to be opened.

I was once such a student. The first time I encountered Dr. Pratt, I thought I was already as opened as one could be. I had long since freed myself from the medievalism of my childhood. I had been in the army and lived abroad. I had seen violence and death. I was married. I had gone to college late and thought I understood what was up by the time I started graduate school in the late 1980s.

Dr. Pratt helped me see that I had simply left one fundamentalism for another. I had moved from relying on Holy Writ to relying on Holy Reason, and the difference between the two was far less radical than I had thought. Both assumed a stable, knowable world. Neither, therefore, understood that the god of this world is Proteus the shape-changer, giver of multiplicity.

Dr. Pratt was always kind to me—and I greatly needed kindness. I am, as I said, not entirely well—"a sort of sick" as Ahab said. I carry the wounds of Adam—that orchard thief—like everyone. But I have a few that Adam knew nothing about. They have not been enough up to now to kill me, but they have kept me swimming in circles most of my life, like a whale with one flipper. And now the voices again.

I don't know whether Dr. Pratt saw that in me back then or not, but he seemed to offer a kind of salve for my wounds. I was bound up, and he spoke of freedom. I was mournful, and he talked about play. I had no center, and he offered the possibility that having no center might be a good thing. Dr. Pratt gave me a new way of explaining my life to myself—or perhaps he simply made me feel better about having no explanation. Either way, I was grateful. And maybe that gratitude explains my finding myself, a few months after his death, standing at his front door, despite an ache in my stomach and a damp, drizzly feeling in my soul.

Judy smiled the whole way over in the car, but puts on her game face when I ring the doorbell. Mrs. Pratt answers and invites us in. She is still attractive, but has been introduced to middle age. She doesn't exactly have lines in her face, but you can see where they're going to be soon enough.

She looks quizzically at Judy as we come in, but receives her graciously. Judy is all formality and soberness.

"My name is Judith Mote. I am here with … I should say, with my brother, Jon."

"Glad to meet you, Judith."

"And you, I am sure."

I haven't seen Mrs. Pratt since I dropped out of graduate school years ago. She was quite a bit younger than Pratt. She won't be a widow for long, unless she wants to be.

Judy sits beside me on the "don't sit on me" white sofa, her feet not quite reaching the floor. I talk generally with Mrs. Pratt about the possibility of working for her. I try to be discouraging, something I'm quite good at.

"What do the police think about me working on the case?"

"I haven't told them. I didn't know if you were going to agree to it."

"They won't like it."

"Why not?"

"It's a vote of no confidence, sort of like showing up at your girlfriend's house for supper carrying a bag of cheeseburgers."

"Well, I *don't* have any confidence. My husband was murdered months ago and they've made no progress at all."

"I understand your frustration, Mrs. Pratt. But it's highly unlikely I would do any better. Those people are professionals. I've never been part of a criminal case before. I work with civil cases, and then only in the background. My last case was eight months ago, and it had to do with a patent infringement for microwave popcorn. Do you see what I mean? I research things like the history of popcorn. I don't know anything about criminal science, or forensics or poisons or weapons, or anything. I don't even know anything about the law—indictments, grand juries, the rules of evidence. None of that."

I want to add, "I can never figure out Sherlock Holmes stories until the last paragraph. Even Watson catches on before I do." But I hold that back.

"Mr. Mote, my husband was a good man. He didn't deserve to have his life end this way. I believe that whoever killed Richard knew him and knew the academic world. You knew Richard, and you know about the academic world. I believe you could pick up on something the police would miss. I would simply like you to look into things and see what you find."

"I'm just afraid you'll be wasting your money. I don't want to raise any false hopes."

"My life is one long lesson in false hopes, Mr. Mote. Don't worry. Even if you find nothing, I'll feel better for your having tried."

I look at Judy. Unfortunately, she takes it as a signal that she should say something.

"Sister Brigit says we … we should always try. If … if … at first you don't sneeze, try … I should say, try, try again." She flashes me a big, how-do-you-like-them-apples smile and then resumes her formal face for Mrs. Pratt.

Mrs. Pratt interprets my not saying no as an indication that I am saying yes, a mistake the women in my life have often made.

"Just for background, let me tell you something that very few people at the university know. I am not Richard's first wife. He first married when he was very young. She was a high school sweetheart. He went to college but she never did. They got married a few days after their high school graduation. She was cute but not, I used to think, very bright. It was a strange match. But of course he wasn't the same person then that he became later.

"His first full-time teaching job was at Memphis State—I think they've changed the name recently. He was there three years, teaching four courses each term, trying to write scholarly articles so he could escape the place, and just failing to live on an assistant professor's salary. Completely overloaded. His wife sat home and dusted their thrift store furniture and waited dutifully and expectantly for the children to start coming. She never knew he was mixing birth control pills in with the vitamins he insisted she take every morning. Poor woman couldn't figure out why she was gaining weight.

"Like I said, I used to think she wasn't very bright. I realized later I never gave her enough credit. I ran into her every once in a while after Richard and I were married. It was strange. She spoke very civilly. I got the distinct impression she felt sorry for me. It was clear she wasn't as dull-witted as I had thought. And she wrote me a very perceptive letter last summer after Richard's death."

"Perceptive?"

"Oh, just about how Richard was, not about anything related to his death. I'm telling you this because I want you to know everything that might be helpful."

We talk for a few minutes more about the little she knows about Pratt's hometown and first marriage; then Mrs. Pratt pauses.

"There's one more relevant thing I think you should know from the start."

I raise my eyebrows, trying to look as professional and encouraging as possible.

"Something was bothering Richard in the last month before his death. Bothering him tremendously. He wouldn't say what it was. In fact, he wouldn't even admit that anything *was* bothering him. But I'm his wife. I could read him like he could decipher a text, and I know for certain that he was greatly troubled. If we could find out what it was, I think we'd know why my husband is dead."

I shoot Judy a stern look to forestall any of Sister Brigit's insights about the dead. That Pratt was troubled by something is not exactly a hot lead, but maybe his state of mind is the best I'm going to get at this point. Since Mrs. Pratt has assumed I will accept her offer, I decide not to fight it.

"Well, Mrs. Pratt, if you think it would be helpful, I'm willing to see what I can come up with. We'll just take it week to week. You tell me to stop anytime you want. I'll bill you every two weeks."

"That's good, Mr. Mote. When do you think you can start?"

"I can start right now."

"Good."

"So there was something bothering your husband. Do you think there was also a who?"

"Yes. Professor Abramson."

FOUR

When I asked Mrs. Pratt why she wanted me to start with Daniel Abramson, she looked away and sighed. She said she liked him very much, but there had been some unpleasantness between him and her husband before Abramson's abrupt retirement the previous year. She said Pratt hadn't talked about it with her, but had alluded to it obliquely a couple of times, saying something about "doing what I have to do for the good of the department," and how it was the worst part of his job. She didn't know anything more specific, but thought it was a place to start.

It certainly wasn't where I wanted to start. I had taken a class or two from Professor Abramson when I was at the university and thought highly of him. He was definitely old school—the gentleman scholar, highly cultured, fluent in five languages, careful in speech and dress, a man who had put all his faith and hope and love into the life of the mind and the imagination. Abramson had emigrated from Budapest shortly after the end of World War II. Apparently he'd hidden out during the war, posing as a pre-seminary student at a Catholic monastery near Szentendre. He got his PhD at Columbia in the 1950s and had been at the University of Minnesota ever since.

Professor Abramson made a big impression on me when I was a student. He approached each work we studied like a shy lover, quietly praising its form and vision. Sometimes he would close his eyes and repeat from memory the words of the text (in the original language), letting their caressing rhythm flow over him. To tell the truth, it embarrassed us. We would exchange looks and suppress smiles. But I have to say that secretly I admired the hell out of the guy. It must be great to love something that much, to find it that important. Why, he loved Tolstoy more than I ever loved my wife (and I still do love her).

Dr. Pratt loved literature too, but in a different way—more like a mistress than a wife. He once said language performed a kind of Dance of the Seven Veils—now revealing, now concealing; exciting us here, disappointing us there, but ultimately just an illusion, nothing more than a tease. Shakespeare, apparently, was the verbal equivalent of Little Egypt.

And if words were ephemeral for Pratt, so were convictions. He changed his positions more often than a runway model changes clothes. He didn't have principles, he had attitudes. Better, he had moods. He took positions on things as his humors dictated, but could melt away from them like butter on a hot skillet, melting words and ideas providing the slippery slide of his escape.

There is room for both Pratt and Abramson in the universe, but they did not coexist all that comfortably in the same building. By the time I was at the U, Abramson's star had set, though he was still respected. Sort of like a former racehorse too old now even for stud, but put out to pasture to enjoy his dotage. His book on the impact of the scientific revolution on literature and art in the seventeenth and eighteenth centuries had been a standard for twenty years. It was said he had turned down offers from Johns Hopkins and Berkeley to stay in Minnesota. He directed so many dissertations that he had to turn students away.

But things had changed by my time, and more rapidly since. He was eased out of the department chairmanship, on the grounds that he deserved more time to write. He found, as his own peers began to retire, that he was increasingly outvoted on new appointments. He vigorously protested a revamping of the curriculum to emphasize "cultural studies," but lost in a landslide. Fewer students signed up for his seminars, fewer still asked him to direct their theses and dissertations. The invitations to speak at conferences dried up, the prestigious journals were politely uninterested in his articles, his dog no longer ran to the door when he came home.

It feels more than strange to be going back to the Humanities building at the university—Abramson still has a small office there even after his retirement. I haven't been back since the day I had my career-ending conversation with Dr. Pratt. The place is definitely haunted.

I leave Judy in the English lounge, where she sits herself down at one end of an abused sofa and pronounces herself right at home.

"You go ahead and talk … I should say, talk to your friend. I will stay here with my own self and … and … watch the world go by." It's a phrase our mom used a lot, and Judy laughs with pleasure to have pulled it out at an appropriate time. Judy's fondness for cliché is positively ontological. Clichés provide a kind of conversational proof that the universe is ordered. Clichés are something you can depend on.

I had called Professor Abramson and explained why I wanted to see him, but neither of us really knows why I am in his office. He greets me very politely and asks how I'm doing. I can tell he is searching my face to see if he remembers me. Heaven knows I never gave him any reason to. I wrote a few indifferent papers for him, took my indifferent grade, and proceeded on with my indifferent life. If he remembers me, it is in the same way one remembers the melting point of copper—a bit of stray information tangled up in a random ganglia in one of the minor folds of the brain.

"Yes, Mr. Mote, I recall your paper on the varying levels of consciousness in the narrative voice in Kundera."

"You do?" I barely remember the paper myself.

"Well, I won't claim to recall the details, but I remember thinking it showed a kind of rough promise."

Rough promise. That was as upbeat an assessment of my life as I'd heard in a long time.

"I'm glad you thought so. Not a promise kept, I'm afraid."

"Oh, I don't know. Promises sometimes get fulfilled in unexpected ways."

I want to get off my life and onto Pratt's death, so I abandon transitions and make a leap.

"As I explained on the phone, Professor Abramson, Mrs. Pratt has asked me to talk to people here at the university to see if anyone might know something that would be helpful to the police in solving Dr. Pratt's death."

"His murder."

"Well, yes, his murder."

"One doesn't solve death, does one? One solves a mystery or a crime."

"Right. I guess no one has solved death, have they? Sorry."

Abramson smiles faintly. I already regret accepting this job. When you're looking into the popping rates of popcorn, no one looks through your eyes into the hollowness of your soul. You just deal with information, not motivation, not implication—not, for heaven's sake, murder.

As is his custom, Professor Abramson senses my discomfort and tries to relieve it.

"Please forgive me for being pedantic, Mr. Mote. You can appreciate that we are still upset here about what happened. We not only lost a valued colleague in a terrible way, we are also a little worried for ourselves."

"Why is that?"

"Until they know who killed Dr. Pratt, we can't be sure it isn't someone who would like to do the same thing to the rest of us."

"The rest of who?" (Or should it be whom?)

"The English faculty. Or anyone here at the university for that matter. Things have changed since I began in the profession. It's a much more … contentious place, as perhaps you noticed even when you were here."

He is being careful. He is by nature reticent and doesn't know how open to be with me, neither a student nor a colleague.

"How so?"

"It used to be you could argue about whether Milton ruined English poetry and then walk across the street and have a beer together. It was a difference of ideas, not of a clash of worldviews. Now everyone has an enemies list."

"Enemies list?"

You can tell he wishes he hadn't said it.

"Well, that's too strong of course. It's just that we used to divide ourselves by specialty or even century—Victorians, medievalists, Shake-spearians—and we could talk to each other. Now we divide by ideology and politics and causes and we are infused with suspicion. It's ironic, Mr. Mote. We have never been so opposed to talking about the moral dimension of literature, and yet we have never been more moralistic and judgmental. And whom do we judge most harshly? The great writers and thinkers of the past. They were, we convince ourselves, little more than imperialists, abusers of women, exploiters of the poor, defenders of a corrupt status quo. Their poems and novels and plays, once thought to be works of genius and insight and wisdom, are now paraded about like handcuffed prisoners being carted to the guillotine. And we, the teachers and scholars, lead the young in howling our abuse."

Professor Abramson has picked up a small bust of Bartók from his desk and is rotating it in his hands. He is conducting, for the thousandth time, a painful conversation within himself, and the outcome can only be sorrowful.

"Not, of course, that any of this leads to murder. But combine an atmosphere of accusation and suspicion with a student who is running up huge tuition bills and has been abandoned by his girlfriend and who believes all the latest conspiracy theories and has just had his dissertation rejected and … ."

Abramson stops abruptly, as though suddenly aware of my presence.

"I apologize. I'm getting carried away. As I said, we are all upset at Dr. Pratt's death, and maybe a bit paranoid."

"I understand completely. It has to be a difficult time for everyone. If I may, I'd like to talk a bit more about this idea of an 'enemies list.'"

"I've exaggerated that. It's really very civil around here most of the time. Everyone acts correctly. We smile at each other in the hallways. The academy gets attacked enough from outsiders, and I don't want to contribute to that."

"What kind of relationship did you have with Dr. Pratt?"

There it is—out on the table, a little too bluntly I fear, but no taking it back. I hate that I used the word "relationship" with Professor Abramson.

It is a squishy, abstract, shop-worn word from our pop psych culture, and it comes out on its own.

"Our relationship, as you call it, was as it should be. He was chair of the department and I respect that position—a position I once held myself, by the way. Most people here do not recall that I was chair when Dr. Pratt was first hired. In fact, I cast the deciding vote in his favor. He was young and inventive and energetic, and we needed all those things at the time.

"And his career subsequently has proven that we made the right choice. He published three widely acclaimed books. He made himself a recognized force among the guerilla avant-garde of the profession, and he brought a lot of grants and attention to a somewhat tired English department, which in recent years he had almost entirely reshaped."

That is a fine summary of Dr. Pratt's career for a speaker's introduction, but it evades the thrust of my question. How do you get a naturally reserved Hungarian-born, war-seared, library-dusty scholar of Eastern European literature to talk to someone like me about his re-la-tion-ship with a dead colleague with whom he was, apparently, in conflict?

That's easy—you keep asking transparently stupid questions in transparently awkward ways.

"Did you and Dr. Pratt get along?"

Abramson shifts in his chair and pauses a long time before answering.

"I would like to be helpful, Mr. Mote, but I am not one to analyze professional relationships in the terms you are suggesting. As I said, I helped hire Dr. Pratt, I watched with some amazement the unfolding of his highly visible career, and I lament very much and very sincerely the ending of his life. It was no secret in the department that he and I had very different understandings of literature and life and of the direction of our profession. But that is, as I said earlier, the nature of academic life today. I may wish things were otherwise, but I do not find many allies in the academy, and I am too old to tilt at windmills. Nevertheless, and this is the point most relevant for your purposes, I most certainly have never wished any of my colleagues ill."

He starts gathering some papers on his desk and putting them into his briefcase.

I want to assure him that I know, of course, that he himself has never wished any harm on Dr. Pratt. I want to say that I am only wondering if he knows of anyone else, student or colleague or janitor, who might have been upset with Pratt. But I know the interview is over even before he stands up and holds out his hand.

"I'm sorry, Mr. Mote. Even though my teaching career is over, I am still writing and I need to go to the library. I wish I could have been of more help. It was good to see you again. If anything pertinent comes to mind, I will be sure to inform you."

When I return to the English lounge, I find Judy deep in conversation with an unusually attractive young woman with dark hair and tusk-white skin. She is sitting next to Judy on the sofa, each turned toward the other as though they are sharing secrets.

Judy spots me over the woman's shoulder and flashes me that bright, puppy-dog look she gives when pleased. Then she launches into one of her laboriously formal introductions:

"Well, there you are, Jon. I want … I should say, I want you to meet my new friend, Miss Bri … Miss Brianna Jones."

Miss Jones, indeed. I offer my hand as she rises from the couch.

"Brianna, this is my … my brother of mine, Mr. Jon Mote."

We exchange greetings as Judy beams from the sofa, satisfied that she has once again successfully navigated another of life's shoals.

"Your sister was just telling me that you used to teach here."

"Oh no, no. I was a graduate student here once. No. I never even finished. I was a grad school dropout."

"Well, I'm about to join those ranks myself. I was telling Judith that I'm here to close out my accounts."

"Have you finished a degree or are you taking a break?"

She looks out the window.

"Well, I've finished something, but it wasn't a degree."

She seems sort of upset. I've been around upset women enough to pick up on the signs. My wife used to send out more distress signals than a sinking ship. But have you ever tried reading signal flags at a thousand yards? There was lots of waving and gesturing, but what the hell was she trying to say? "Abandon ship"? "Come on board"? "Torpedoes off the starboard bow"? Not being much good at the hermeneutics of female cues, I usually just sat there, contemplating the cold Atlantic waves.

This time, I pull anchor.

"It's been nice meeting you, Brianna. Let's go Judy. We've got to get home."

It takes a three count for Judy to process that it's time to go and then notify her body.

"Yes, Jon. I ... I am coming. I am coming right now."

She gets her feet on the ground, bends at almost a right angle, and pushes herself slowly away from the sofa. She carefully pulls down her sweater, straightens her shoulders, and holds out her hand to her new friend.

"It has been nice talk ... talking with you, Bri ... Brianna Jones. I am ... I should say, I am very glad to have made your acquaintance."

Brianna returns the formality. "And yours as well, Judith. I hope we see each other again in the future."

This delights Judy to no end.

"Yes, perhaps on ... on another occasion."

Since this exchange has no guaranteed ending point, I take Judy by the hand and we head out the door.

FIVE

Outside the Humanities building, I'm starting to feel unwell. I have levels of unwellness, ranging from the generic to the acute. This unwellness is more specific than usual.

I reach into my jacket pocket for some of my pills, but come up empty. Something is going on in my mind, and it portends nothing good. I shouldn't have come back here. It's like a geriatric Napoleon signing up for a senior citizen bus tour of Waterloo. I mean, why spread out your picnic blanket on the freeway? You're just begging the universe to notice you—never a good thing.

I don't do too well with the past. I don't know why. Maybe it's that the past is never actually past. Nothing is ever over, ever finished, ever gone. It's like with garbage. There's really no "away" in "throw away." Everything goes *some*where—"away" just means out of sight, not out of existence. You can stick something in a barrel, or cover it up with dirt, or drop it in an ocean canyon. But it's still *there*. Even burning something up doesn't really make it go "away"; it merely changes its configuration, rearranges atoms.

And if it's true with candy bar wrappers and toxic waste, how much more so with toxic memories?

During the ride back to the houseboat, Judy is basking in the afterglow of her new friendship.

"Brianna reminds me of my … my Sunday school teacher of mine."

I know Judy hasn't been to any Sunday school since she's been back with me, so I'm prepared for her to dredge up any of the dozen teachers she must have had as a girl. For her the saying "It's like it was yesterday" is literally true. Her mind makes no significant distinction between earlier today and thirty-five years ago. She cannot remember that three plus four equals seven, but recalls every word our mother said to her when the ice cream fell out of her cone when she was five.

"Which Sunday school teacher was that, Jude?"

"Miss Sinclair. You remember her, Jon. She is my favorite. I ... I like her very much."

I don't remember Miss Sinclair, of course. I do remember Sunday school. Sunday school marked one of the first encounters with the problem of evil for little fundamentalist children like me. How can a good God have created a world in which innocent kids have to go to Sunday school? Was God just not powerful enough to prevent Sunday school, or was he not totally good?

Sunday school in my day was low-tech flannel board presentations by high-anxiety teachers like Mr. Ring: "Here, children, is Joseph in his coat of many colors. You all have a picture of Joseph wearing his coat in your workbooks. I want you to take that home and color it and bring it back next Sunday and you will get twenty points. Now remember that the two students who earn the most points this quarter get to go with me to play putt-putt golf and have a hamburger at The Flame. But I don't want to see any of you coloring that coat in the service next hour. You are old enough now to listen to Pastor Patterson's sermon. Barry, I saw you laying your head in your mother's lap last week. Don't you think you're a little too big for that? Now here is the well Joseph's brother threw him in. Why do you think they did that, children? Why did they throw Joseph in the well? Yes, Barry... . No, Barry, it wasn't because he didn't believe in Jesus. Jesus comes later. Yes, Cecil... . That's right. They were jealous of him. What does it mean to be jealous, children? Are you ever jealous? When might you be jealous? That's right, Arnie—when your brother hits a home run in Little League and everybody thinks he's so great. Yes, Barry? ... Why yes, the Bible does say God is a jealous God.

No, Barry, it doesn't mean God has sinned. It's different. God doesn't sin. Yes, I understand that if something's wrong, it's wrong. But it isn't the same thing. It's … well, something you boys are too young to understand right now. We can talk about it later."

It wasn't Mr. Ring's fault. All week long he sold auto parts. It was nothing but tie rods and head gaskets and spark gap setters. How was he supposed to know why God was allowed to be jealous when we shouldn't be? And how was he supposed to teach eight kinetic third-grade boys the Bible on Sunday when he didn't know anything about teaching and had only volunteered because the Sunday school superintendent had made him feel guilty that no one else would? And maybe because his own son had died at age four and would have been the same age as these boys, and there was an empty spot in his heart that some unconscious part of him thought they could fill.

It amazes me now that we never questioned the whole enterprise. We went to Sunday school the way salmon go home to spawn—relentlessly, unreflectively, as part of our nature. It's spawning season—the salmon must get home. It's Sunday morning—I must hie me to Sunday school. I must be here with Mr. Ring and Joseph's coat of many colors. I must figure out, somehow, what this story has to do with me—with playing outside, and school, and my dark, secret thoughts.

secret for now

It's hard for me to believe I was ever part of such a world. I wonder if Sunday school even exists anymore. It's been so many years since I've gone to church that I have a hard time remembering exactly what goes on there. Can little kids, somewhere, still be singing, "Red and yellow, black and white, they are precious in his sight"? Are there still cannibals in the world?

"Miss Sinclair is very nice to me."

I keep driving.

"She said I looked … looked pretty in my Easter dress of mine."

I feel a stab in my stomach. Now I remember Miss Sinclair. She was a high school girl who was very active in the church and was later killed in a car wreck. She had been especially good to Judy.

I remember that Easter dress, too. She must have been ten or eleven. It was an archetype—or parody—of the genre of cute, petticoated, wavy-rufflely little girl dresses. Judy loved the showers of praise and admiration from Dad when she walked down the steps from her bedroom wearing it, Mother trailing behind and clearing her throat to make sure the men of the house took proper note. Dad claimed not to recognize her.

"Where's Judy? Miss Princess, could you tell me where my daughter Judy has gone?"

Judy immediately struck a pose, aloof and regal.

"Why, I … why, I am your very own daughter, Judy."

"No, my daughter is very pretty, of course, but you are the most lovely woman in the world. You cannot be my daughter."

"Yes, I … I am lovely. But I am also your daughter … Judith Anne Mote. How do you like my … my new dress of mine?"

If Judy got praise for her dress at home, she got a few stares at church. In those days you didn't call attention to a tragedy, maybe even to a judgment of God. For some it was a scandal that she still lived at home, a situation that would change soon enough.

By the time we get home from the university, I can feel the first dimming of the light. I refuse it the encouragement of direct attention. I tell myself I am simply tired, which is true enough. I know for sure I shouldn't have agreed to look into Pratt's murder. Too many ghosts at the university. They linger in the seminar rooms and library stacks—patient, vaporous, not quite sinister, not quite friendly. At best they wish me no particular good. They are better left alone and at a distance, like the rumor of faraway disaster.

we wish you no particular good either

I try talking to Judy to keep my thoughts from turning inward, but I'm having a hard time paying attention. While her words pile up on her tongue like rush hour traffic, I am drawn to the dark edge of the mind where thought descends into randomness and randomness into emptiness and emptiness into oblivion. I feel an overwhelming need to escape the press of judgment and evaluation. I don't exactly want to sleep. I want to absent myself from the world for a while. It isn't a new feeling, but one I haven't felt this strongly for a long time. It is a feeling I have never been good at resisting, or even wanting to resist. I tell Judy I am going to lay on the couch for a few minutes. She looks alarmed.

SIX

The next day I go down to the Minneapolis police headquarters between Fourth and Fifth streets to introduce myself to Detective Wilson, the lead detective on the case. The headquarters are in city hall, which looks appropriately authoritative, like a cross between a grand French chateau and the witch's fortress in *The Wizard of Oz*. Mrs. Pratt called Detective Wilson after our meeting to let him know about me, and it has had the effect I expected. When I appear in his office he looks at me like a father looks at a biker picking up his daughter for a first date.

"I may as well tell you right out that I don't like this."

"I understand."

"But Mrs. Pratt has the right to hire whoever she wants."

"Yes."

"*As long as* that person doesn't get in the way of the investigation."

"Of course."

"Or break any laws."

"I understand."

"Including laws of privacy and search and seizure."

"Of course."

"You are not a cop, and I don't want you playing cop. If you leave anyone with even the faintest impression that you are an officer or in any way connected to the official investigation …"

"You'll have no problem …"

"I will charge your ass."

"… with me."

"And if you should by absolute random luck come across anything—and I mean *anything*—I want to hear about it before your next breath."

He pauses, standing behind his desk, leaning forward on his knuckles.

"Do I make myself clear."

"As a bell." Cliché answering cliché. Judy would be proud.

"Is there any more I can do for you, Mr. Mote?"

This normally would be my cue for a mumbled exit line and a quick departure. I stand up to do just that when I see something in a plastic bag on top of a stack of papers on the edge of Wilson's desk that makes my heart jump. It looks like a knife, but I instantly know it isn't a knife—I know what it is instead.

"What is that?"

long time no see

Wilson looks where I'm pointing and snorts. He takes the bag and drops it into a drawer.

"That's none of your business, that's what it is."

"It's the murder weapon, isn't it?"

Suddenly Wilson is keenly interested.

"And how would you know that, Mr. Mote?"

"I've seen it before."

Now Wilson is more than interested; he's riveted.

"That is indeed the weapon Dr. Pratt was attacked with. But the public doesn't know that. We disclosed that Dr. Pratt was stabbed, but we didn't describe the weapon. We let people assume it was a knife, so we could distinguish a false confession from a true one. Mrs. Pratt doesn't even know. If you've seen it before, Mr. Mote, then I think perhaps I should read you your Miranda rights."

It isn't a knife. It's a gold letter opener. The blade is narrow, about nine inches long. But it's the handle that's distinctive. It's a whale. In fact, it's Moby Dick. Its golden head and body form the handle, and the blade of the opener comes out its tail.

I know the murder weapon, and I know it's Moby Dick because years ago Pratt pulled it out of his briefcase one day as class was beginning. He held it up for all to see and performed one of his sixty-second, spontaneous tours de force that left you amazed—at how brilliant he was and how brilliant you weren't.

"This letter opener, students, is a perfect exemplum of the derivative and allusive nature of all that we so innocently call 'reality.' It purports to be an opener of letters. Simple enough. But it has a whale for a handle. And not just any whale. This whale is Moby Dick, of literary fame. How do I know this is Moby Dick? Because I bought it myself at Melville's home in Pittsfield, Massachusetts. No whale within a hundred miles of Pittsfield can be any other than Moby Dick. Not in the mind of the purveyor of the whale, nor in the mind of the viewer. History and biography and culture have colluded to equate Pittsfield with Melville and Melville with whale and whale with Moby Dick.

"But of course this is not a whale at all. It's a piece of cheap pot metal, painted gold. It is merely an iconographic representation of a whale. And it's certainly not the specific whale Moby Dick. Not only because a whale is flesh and blood and this whale is metal and paint, but because the whale Moby Dick never existed in time and space. Moby Dick never got wet, never ate a squid, never did any whaley things, because it existed only in the mind of Herman Melville. And Melville turned that mental Moby Dick into little black squiggles on a white piece of paper. And those little alphabetic symbols arbitrarily suggest to us 'whale,' a highly improbable creature most people have never actually seen with their own eyes but that they are nonetheless certain exists.

"So, this whale-handled letter opener is really a symbol of a symbol of a symbol, the grounds of which were electrochemical discharges in Melville's brain—whoever Melville was (as if we could ever really know). And that's not even to mention the person who decided to manipulate this symbol for profit, making this tawdry little curio for bookish tourists, most of whom read novels with the naiveté of children—capitalism again reducing everything it touches to quid pro quo, simplifying the playful complexities of art to the periodic elements of dollars and cents."

See what I mean? Pratt took your black-and-white, monochromatic world and gave you back a kaleidoscope of colorful, if fleeting, connections. And you thought it was a simple letter opener. Ha!

Seeing the letter opener now, I feel more grief for Dr. Pratt than I had even at the time of his death. Symbol of a symbol of a symbol? Perhaps, but also sharp enough to have made a very effective hole in you, sir—the revenge of simple materiality over all things theoretical.

I give Detective Wilson the short version of all this, assuring him that hundreds of people had seen that letter opener over the years in Pratt's classes. I can't tell whether he believes me or not, but he doesn't read me my rights. He settles for a simple threat.

"You shouldn't have seen that. If I hear anywhere that the murder weapon was other than a knife, I will know that you are the source of that information and I will charge you with obstructing the investigation. Understand?"

I assure him that I do. And I remember Pratt's words that day in class as he put the letter opener back in his briefcase.

"I always carry this with me to remind myself that everything we experience is actually a quotation of something else—something only slightly less unreal. And also to fend off attacks from my rival critics!"

We all laughed then, but now it doesn't seem so funny.

we think its hilarious

SEVEN

Judy sits in the car while I get my warm welcome from Detective Wilson. She greets my return with her best smile.

"Well, Jon, how … I should say, how did it go with Mr. … with Mr. Dick Tracy?" She laughs at her cleverness, and I can't help but join her.

"It went fine, Jude. He hates that I'm involved and he promises to send me to jail if I mess things up."

"That is not … I should say, very very nice."

"No, not nice. But I don't blame him. If I don't find anything useful, then I'm just another irritation on an irritating case. And if I do, then he looks incompetent. I know the feeling."

"Billy was in … incompetent. Sister Brigit said so. He had to wear diapers."

I let that pass.

As I pull away from the curb, Judy reminds me to buckle my seat belt. She is very legalistic about seat belts, as she is about cigarettes, prayer before meals, sharp objects, bad words, hot stoves, saying please and thank you, brushing your teeth up and down not back and forth, taking your shoes off at the door, setting the table, and too much television. In short, she can be a real pain.

Before we go back to the boat, I've got to pick up a part for the stove at Dey's Appliance on Snelling and then make another stop further north at HarMar Mall. So I take 94 to Snelling and go up to Dey's. After getting the part, I continue north, negotiating with my thoughts, when Judy suddenly sits up as tall as she can, lifting her eyes above the bottom of the window like a prairie dog looking out its burrow.

"That's where my daddy of mine takes me for choc ... choc ... chocolate dips."

I snap to attention, suddenly and inexplicably nervous. I see the entrance to the state fairgrounds. We have crossed the Rubicon, unawares, into our old neighborhood. In an instant I am taken back to my childhood. Our house was only a few blocks from the fairgrounds. Our parents took us to the fair every year and, as part of the ritual, Dad always bought Judy a vanilla cone dipped in chocolate.

"You're right, Jude. We used to get ice cream there, didn't we?"

"Yes ... yes we did, Jon. That is where my very own daddy of mine takes me for choc ... chocolate dips."

We sit at a red light for a few seconds in silence.

"I ... I ... I miss my daddy very much."

I don't have anything to say. Our father has been dead for going on thirty years now. How can you miss something you hardly remember having? I was only nine when he died. Judy was thirteen. If it wasn't for photographs, I couldn't tell you what he looked like—though I have a feeling his photographs don't do him justice. I mean, what are photographs anyway? Thousands of little dots of color—or shades of gray. Arrange the dots just so and you fool the eye into thinking it's *seeing* something, something from the real world. But it's just dots. We know this, but we agree to fool ourselves. We agree to play along, to pretend we're seeing something real.

Come to think of it, the camera only does what the eye itself does first. Our brain sits in splendid isolation, taking in data from the field—from the eyes, the nose, the tongue, the ears, and other scattered parts. The eye receives photons of light bouncing off everything out there, which are converted into electrical impulses and sent along the optic nerve to the brain. Then the brain takes the impulses, throws most of them away, and sorts the rest, transmuting the agitated electrons into a "picture" of the world. And we all agree to participate in the illusion that this picture is Reality.

Yikes! Pratt isn't dead. He's alive and well in my overheated brain.

When I make a mistake, like allowing the car to take me here, I tend to make another to keep it company. Mistakes need friends, just as we all do. And so I glance over at Judy.

"How about it, Jude. Since we're close to the old neighborhood, what say we drive by our house?"

Judy shoots me a baleful look, but doesn't reply.

"Let's just drive by and take a look. I haven't seen the place in years."

I turn right two blocks on and head into another haunted part of town, a place you can't get to by roads alone.

The closer we get to our old street (named after a French philosopher no less, a fellow who knew a thing or two about the void) the less believable everything seems. The Mdewakanton Dakota used to pass through here on their way to collecting wild rice on lakes a bit north, but the present neighborhood was mostly built in the 1920s and '30s. Tall shade trees once lined the streets, but Dutch elm disease has killed off most of them. The few left behind look skeletal and misplaced, like the odd rotten tooth in a mostly toothless mouth. We turn onto our old street and I start scanning for our house, pretending to be casual. Judy scrunches down in her seat, refusing to look.

"Well, there she is, Jude," I say breezily as I pull the car up to the curb. I don't feel breezy. Judy peeps over the bottom edge of the car window, like a soldier in a trench wary of snipers. It occurs to me that she likely hasn't been here since shortly after Mom and Dad's funeral. We walked out of the house a few weeks later, each carrying a suitcase, headed for Uncle Lester's. And Judy has never been back, not until just now. No wonder she's lying low.

The house looks strangely innocent, all whitish stucco, wrought iron, and one upstairs shuttered window by the chimney, but I know better. In my mind I walk myself up to the rounded front door—think ovens—and through the entryway into the living room on the right. Nothing has changed. Hardwood floors, gapped but shiny. A motley collection of furniture, not quite comfortable anymore, but too familiar to consider replacing. My father's stuffed chair, the right arm darkened from years of buttered popcorn. In the corner by the window is the small, primitive television. It was old and outdated by the time I came along, but it had caused a stir when my parents got it, one of the first families in the church to get one. The pastor made it clear he didn't think televisions belonged in a Christian home. My mother told him a lot of Christians she knew didn't belong in a Christian home either. At least that's what Aunt Wanda reported years later when I asked what my mother was like.

I see my parents and us watching reruns of *The Honeymooners*. "Bang, zoom, straight to the moon, Alice!" We don't know enough to be offended. My dad laughs every time Norton comes into the room. Says he used to have a hat like that when he was a kid.

On the walls cheap prints compete with even cheaper studio photographs of the family. No one looks believable. Our skin sort of glows, like those plastic Santas with a light bulb screwed into their backs. And then there are the portraits of the dead. The faces are colored a kind of buttered-toast gold. You can't imagine any of them ever telling a joke or sneaking a drink.

The snapshots are more compelling. Here's Grandpa Nick as a young man among his co-workers in the oil fields of Southern California. He stands on the platform of a well, short and stocky, the collar of his shirt open and a confident look in his eyes. He's just back from kicking the Kaiser's butt in France and looks ready to do the same to life in general.

And yet, by the time I first saw that photograph, Grandpa Nick was already dead. Heart attack in his forties. I could never quite reconcile the living figure in the photograph, all breath and expectation, with the knowledge that he was dead and disintegrated long before I was even born. It seemed to me that this photograph somehow kept him alive—or at least in existence—and I worried that we were too casual with it, letting it just hang there by the entryway, liable to disasters of every kind.

In my mind I walk through the living room, turning left into the small dining room that joined it at right angles. We only sat at the dining room table on Sunday afternoons and when company was over. But all four of us are sitting there now. My mother is instructing Judy.

"If the butter is closer to someone else than it is to you, Judy, you should ask them to pass it, even if you think you can reach it yourself."

My father is telling me he's glad there's a pro baseball team in Minnesota now because he gets to take me to games, like his father did with him when he was a kid.

I drift out of the dining room into the kitchen. The white refrigerator with the rounded corners sits, as it always will, next to the back door. Its long silver spike handle pulls forward like a slot machine. After one summer Bible camp where the speaker dragged us step by bloody step through the crucifixion, I couldn't look at that handle without thinking of giant nails being driven through Jesus' hands. It kept me from looking in the frig for a snack for weeks.

The kitchen table is red, with shiny silver edges and metal legs. The chairs match the table—curved metal with red vinyl seats, split after years of use, the white fibers sticking out like gauze on an open wound. I see oatmeal steaming in a bowl, vapors rising in twining spirals before disappearing in the air.

I lean over the sink and look out the kitchen window into the backyard. Huge. Bigger than it can possibly be. It is terraced, the lawn rolling up higher near the back fence, like old Crosley Field in Cincinnati. I imagine Vada Pinson gliding back to catch a long fly ball against the fence and throwing it back into me at shortstop. I see our dog, Blue, lying in the sun, her tongue hanging out as she pants, at ease, satisfied with her place, without thought for past or future.

I walk out of the kitchen through the second interior door and back into where the entryway meets the living room, facing the front of the house. I turn right down the hallway, and see the two bedroom doors, one on the right and one on the left, at the end of the hall. But as I walk toward them, I come to the steep narrow stairs on my right that lead up to Judy's tiny dormered bedroom.

I look up the stairs and feel a hollowness in my stomach. I see the bookcase at the top of the stairs, filled with the first books that had come to my aid. The bookcase is covered in shadows. In my mind, I try climbing up the stairs, but my feet are heavy, very heavy. My knees will not bend. I somehow get to the first step, then the second. I hear a noise, and the hollowness in my stomach turns to pain.

dont go up there you fool

A squeal comes from the bedroom, like a mouse being crushed by a boot.

run away you coward run away before its too late

Judy grabs my wrist and I look into her terrified eyes. The door to our old house starts to open from inside. I pull the car away from the curb and accelerate down the street like Ichabod before the Headless Horseman.

EIGHT

After the blowback from driving by our old house, it's several days before I'm myself again. Then again, what does that mean, "I'm myself"? Which "myself" is the real one? What is a "self" anyway?

Where's Pratt when you need a good deconstruction?

oh thats right hes dead end of self

I remember him quoting a warning from another Melville novel once, something about being careful about seeking self-knowledge, you may mistake yourself for someone else. I know I have. I mean, I'm pretty sure there's more than one of me. My wife said so. And Uncle Lester before her.

me and my shadow strolling down the avenue

But don't we all have multiple versions of ourselves? Private self, public self, self for the spouse, self for the boss, self for our friends at the pub. And we don't always get to choose which one to be at a given moment. At least I don't. Sometimes life seems to assign me a self and there's not a lot I can do about it. Other times, more than one self shows up.

Like when Uncle Lester caught me and a neighbor boy playing with a ouija board a year or two after Judy and I had moved in with him. Lester ran the kid out of the house and then turned on me, his head full of Leviticus. He unbuckled his belt as he walked toward me, saying something about me being cut off for consulting with mediums and spirits. He liked that phrase, "cut off." He used it a lot. And it was always him doing the cutting and me on the receiving end.

This time he was madder than usual.

"You have contaminated my house. You have brought powers and principalities into my very home. You have turned a godly house into a place for demons. You are possessed of evil spirits. You will be cut off."

I was petrified. I knew it was true. I knew what it felt like to have something else sharing my mind. I was unclean and deserved to be cut off. I even determined to take the whipping without flinching. But when I saw the horrible look on his face as he reached for me, I ran.

He caught me by the back of my shirt. I let my legs go limp so as to fall onto the floor and shrink into the smallest possible target, but he lifted me by the shirt and started whipping me with his belt. Usually I could get away after three or four licks, but this time he had a good hold. He just kept hitting me, over and over. I thought that he might kill me this time. Part of me was attracted to the idea.

Then, suddenly, there were no more licks, and he dropped me to the floor. I slid away and looked back. Judy had grabbed his right arm and wouldn't let it go. He was yelling and cursing at her.

"Don't think I won't whip you too, you little idiot. Let go of my arm, goddamn you."

But Judy wouldn't let go. She had her eyes closed tight and her lips were moving silently. I didn't stay to see what happened next. I ran out the front door and didn't come back until late in the night.

thats right run run wee cowrin timrous beastie let your sister take the heat save your own sorry ass

Living with Uncle Lester was like living in a Kafka novel. Not that I'd heard of Kafka, of course. But when I discovered him later, I knew how his characters felt. The world is full of rules, but it's never clear exactly what they are or how to keep them. Some of Uncle Lester's rules were easy enough: "Don't smoke, don't drink, don't chew—and don't go with girls who do." But others were amorphous and hazy, like "have the mind of Christ," "be godly," and "show thyself approved." And then there were the rules that couldn't be found in the Bible, but that were all the more powerful for being unstated.

I had the distinct feeling I was playing (and losing) a game in which only the umpires know all the rules. Sometimes you learned about a rule only after you'd broken it. Uncle Lester was the umpire in his house—an official representative of the Big Umpire Upstairs—and forgiveness came at the end of a belt, if it came at all.

NINE

I need some time to pull things together, but time is something I don't have. I am out of money, for one, and in America to be out of money is literally to be worthless. No money, no worth, no reason to be. Even *with* money I am short on reasons to be. Add empty pockets to an empty heart and pretty soon you're staring down the barrel of a not-so-empty gun.

The only way to get money, at present, is to keep looking for whoever killed Richard Pratt. I am billing by the hour but dissolving by the minute, and so I get up one Wednesday vowing to get back on the productivity treadmill.

The tread that day leads to Verity Jackson, a woman who made a scene at Pratt's presentation the night he was murdered, thereby making herself a suspect. She had stood up and yelled at Pratt as he wrapped up his talk, and was escorted noisily out of the ballroom. The police, according to Detective Wilson, have interviewed her twice, but haven't filed any charges and are unlikely to now. I'm sure she doesn't have anything to do with killing Pratt, but I don't know of anyone else to talk to and I need the hours.

I call Ms. Jackson at Metro State, where she teaches remedial English, mostly to adults. I expect her to say, "Who are you and why should I talk to you about anything?" Instead, when I mention Mrs. Pratt, she says she'll meet me in Loring Park by the fiddler that afternoon at four. She speaks quietly and politely and briefly. I hang up, first pleased that it had been so easy, then disconcerted when I realize I don't know what I'm going to say to her.

I bring Judy along for protection. We park near the Walker and cut through the sculpture garden. Judy spots the big spoon with the cherry.

"Looks like Mr. ... Mr. Paul Bunyan has been here."

The connection escapes me, like most connections.

We cross over Hennepin Avenue into the park on a pedestrian bridge that tries to be artsy while getting you safely over six lanes of traffic. It sports various phrases from a cryptic poem all the way across. I feel like I'm walking in a Buddhist koan: "What is the sound of one bridge clapping?" My whole life is a koan—long on paradox and brain busters.

The fall is everywhere present. Many of the leaves have already leapt from the trees. Those that remain are mostly yellow and brown, with just a few orange and red dazzlers here and there. The colors are past their peak by a week or two, the remaining leaves holding on now by sheer bravado. I know the feeling. Winter is so inevitable it can afford to dawdle, to allow a few more jacketless walks in the park.

"This is very pretty, Jon. It reminds me of ... of my very own calendar in my bedroom."

Which calendar and which bedroom are anyone's guess. She doesn't have a calendar in her bedroom now. Maybe in her former room at Good Shepherd. Maybe when she was three. Who could tell? She investigates the past like a fly buzzing through the air from point to point, all instant right angles, abrupt changes in elevation, unexpected landings and take-offs. Hers is a random access memory—Judy is the Intel of recall.

We walk around the small lake and past the fountain that looks like a giant wet dandelion. I am thinking of Verity Jackson's name. Who names their kid after a virtue anymore? What's in a name, anyway? Is it just a label, an arbitrary collection of letters and sounds that say "you"? Or is it rooted in something? I mean, does it matter if a kid is named "Candy" or "Brandy" because the parents think it's cute, as opposed to being named, say, "Lydia," after your great aunt Lydia, who was the first woman in the state to get a medical degree and was herself named after the deacon in the New Testament? People used to think your name was your destiny. What's the destiny implied in "Brandy"?

Some tribes used to delay naming newborns for a time so evil spirits couldn't learn their names and get power over them. I like that. I would gladly be nameless even now.

I spot Verity Jackson waiting for us, sitting on a bench near the statue of a large brown fiddler. I had caught a glimpse of her when she was led out at Pratt's talk, but she looks smaller sitting there on the bench than she looked that night.

Ms. Jackson is a black woman of indeterminate age, as many black women are—for me, anyway. She's at least fifty but might be a lot older. She is lean. Her skin is smooth and unwrinkled, but she has just a few strands of gray. Her hair is relatively short and curled under, a sort of old-fashioned look. The main impression she gives is of quiet dignity.

I introduce myself and then Judy. Ms. Jackson seems to relax a bit once she looks into Judy's eyes and shakes her hand.

"Sit here beside me, Judy, and tell me what this brother of yours wants with an old black lady like me."

Judy is eager to tell all.

"Well, my brother ... my brother Jon of mine is ... is like Mr. Perry Como."

I roll my eyes and groan.

"Does he sing then?"

"No ... no wait. I mean ... I mean to say, he is like Mr. Perry Mason."

Damn those reruns. "I'm not like Perry Mason at all. I'm ..."

"My brother talks to people to see ... to see if they have ... have done something wrong."

"I see."

Some sidekick she is. The Lone Ranger would have never put up with this from Tonto.

"But he does ... does not put them, I should say, into jail."

"That's comforting."

"Because, you see, he is not an off ... an officer of the law."

"You might say he's more like a snitch, then, Judy? Would that be right?"

"Why, yes. That sounds right."

Then Judy smiles at me as though to say, "I've done what I can for you, Jon. Now you're on your own."

"So, Mr. Mote, how can I help you?"

I want to say, "You can shoot me and put me out of my misery," but say instead, "I feel like I need to explain."

Ms. Jackson laughs softly and puts her hand on my forearm.

"Mr. Mote, Judy and I are just playing the dozens with you."

Another smile and a nod from Judy.

"I think I know why Mrs. Pratt asked you to look into her husband's death. I would have done the same. And I also know I can't be of much help to you. I got upset that night and did something I'm not proud of. I was raised to be respectful of other people and their views and I should have been more respectful of Dr. Pratt."

"Had you ever met Dr. Pratt before?"

"No, but I have benefited from his kindness."

"How so?"

"I spent most of my adult life working in low-level office jobs. When my last child left home, I decided I had time to better myself. And so I went back to school and finished my college degree and then went straight on and got a master's, and then I landed a job here at Metro and I've been here ever since."

"I would … I would like to say … con … congratulations to you, Ms. Verity Jackson. I would."

"Thank you, Judy. I appreciate that. And I got my master's at the university. I never had a class from Dr. Pratt. In fact, I never even saw him while I was there. It's a very big department, and I had no time to go to events or socialize, and for at least one year he was on a study leave in France."

I remember hearing about that year in France from Pratt himself when I was a student. He talked about it a lot. Said it changed everything for him. It was the year he wrote his breakthrough book. He went away a junior member of the department and came back a rock star in the making. So Ms. Jackson had been at the university only a few years before I came, though apparently she'd arrived both older and wiser than I had.

"I won an award for my master's thesis that year. Dr. and Mrs. Pratt had established a prize for the best thesis each year by a disadvantaged student. It meant a lot to me. It gave me a shot of confidence and a thousand dollars to boot. I remember Mrs. Pratt presented the award to me at a small ceremony. Dr. Pratt was still in France. But she was very kind and told me to keep up the good work."

"That's what ... what Sister Illuminata says when I clean the kitch ... that is, the kitchen. Keep up ... the ... the good work, Judy, she says to me."

Ms. Jackson puts up her hand for a high five and Judy slaps it, then rocks back, rubbing her hands together in delight.

"I wrote to Dr. Pratt, thanking him for sponsoring the award. He replied with a very kind and encouraging letter and an offer to help me in the future. Actually, he helped me get this job here at Metro. Put in a good word for me. I owe both him and Mrs. Pratt a lot."

I don't know exactly how to ask the obvious. If she was on such good terms with Dr. Pratt, why did she make a scene at the end of his talk? Ms. Jackson moves on to the issue without any prompting.

"Yes, I owe him a lot. But in that speech, and, I have to say, in his books too, he asks too much."

"How do you mean? Maybe I'm missing something, but didn't he talk a lot about things like deconstructing systems and hierarchies of power in order to free people of color from bondage, and women from patriarchy, and ... someone or other from something or other?"

"Yes, he did. And there was time in my life when that would have been enough. I would have clapped and cheered with the rest of them."

She looks out over the park and it becomes clear that she is seeing something I can't see.

"Let me just tell you a bit about this park, Mr. Mote. It's called Loring Park now, but it used to be called Central Park. We'd come here for picnics when I was a little girl. It wasn't a place where a black family felt welcome back then. I'm just giving you a little history here. But my mother was the kind of woman to eat her fried chicken wherever she wanted, and this was one of the places she wanted."

"I … I should say … I like fried chicken."

"When I was a little older, I used to come here on dates. I got my first kiss under that big oak over there. Wasn't everyone glad to see us in the park even then, but we weren't necessarily glad to see all of them either.

"And they weren't any happier to see us in the sixties when we came to this park to demonstrate for civil rights and against the war."

Why is she telling me this?

"Then later there were the Take Back the Night rallies. I remember us holding burning torches and listening to speakers and trying to get back that feeling from the sixties and not quite succeeding. But at least we made it clear that we thought a woman should be able to walk around outside after dark. Like I say, I'm just giving you a little history here. Do you understand?"

"I understand."

But I don't understand at all. What does any of this have to do with Pratt, who would have agreed with every cause she mentioned and a dozen more?

"You see, Mr. Mote. This park is full of stories for me. And it's only one place of many. I'm nothing without my stories. I need them all and I need them to be strong and life-sustaining things. How can they be strong, Mr. Mote, if they fall apart so easily in the hands of people like Dr. Pratt? Did you hear *how* he was going to undo empire and patriarchy and homophobia and every other bad thing?"

I waited for her to answer her own question.

"By killing words, Mr. Mote. By denying the ability of words to capture our experience and explain our lives to ourselves. If words are such weak and self-destructing things, then there is no truth, and if no truth, there is only power, and we, of all people, know what it's like to be on the receiving end of power."

Verity Jackson is talking to the ancestors.

"What do poor people have if they don't have words? Do they have tanks? No. Do they have money? No. Do they have the majority of votes? Absolutely no. If they don't have words that can truthfully and powerfully tell their stories—in a way that can change things—they are poor indeed.

"I got angry that night, and I started talking back to him, because Dr. Pratt wasn't just talking against Big Brother and God and most of the writers who have given me hope in life; he was also undermining Martin and Malcolm and Sojourner and Gandhi and anyone else who ever said, 'This is wrong and things should be different.' Words may just be play for him, but they aren't play for people like me who depend on their stories."

We were all silent. Judy came to the rescue.

"I like ... I should say, I like stories very much."

TEN

Having talked with Professor Abramson and Verity Jackson, I have exhausted my suspects list. It's obvious neither of them killed Dr. Pratt or know who did. As usual, I am a man without leads.

And so I do what I often do in this situation. I decide to read. Books were an early lifeline, and I turn to them regularly with a certain desperate hopefulness. People talk about reading as an escape from reality—I tend to think of it as an escape *into* reality. Books aren't an escape from trouble. There's more trouble in novels—and most other books—than anywhere else. Books aren't even an escape from your own particular troubles, because a good book always makes you think about your own life while it pretends to distract you from it.

It's just that books suggest the possibility that trouble can be survived, if you know what I mean. Or at least named. Books are more real for me than the rest of my life because they light up more parts of me than the rest of my life ever has. I mean, you can be little more than a damned cartoon figure and get along quite nicely in life—maybe even become president.

Think about our last few presidents. You don't have to be any high-octane deconstructionist to see that having a movie actor for a president tells us more about ourselves than we want to know. We've had a surfeit of reality and grown sickened. Give us a guy *playing* president anytime over the real thing.

And the current guy, just coming to the end of his run in front of the bright lights, is more of an actor than the actor president was. He knows just when to furrow his brow to look thoughtful, when to bite his lip to look emotional, when to tilt his chin up to look presidential. If he could fool his wife all those years, he can fool us all—and he has. (Though perhaps she was never fooled at all and the last laugh is hers.) And now we're holding our breath to see who the next actor will be.

Maybe every president is playing the role of ... ta da ... *president*! Maybe that's what "president" is—a role to be played, lines to be said, papers to be signed, buttons to be pushed (including, if the script requires, the nuclear one). What is any of us doing but playing a role? Look at me, I'm pretending to be a detective. I once pretended to be a student and a husband. I've got more me's inside than that dog has fleas.

you dont know the half of it

Okay, so I decide to read for a while. But of course I can't bill Mrs. Pratt for reading Dickens. I resolve to do some reading in the recent writings of one Richard Pratt. What had he been thinking in his last months? Who was he doing battle with? What dragons was he slaying that might have bitten back? It is a singularly unpromising path to finding a murderer, but it is attractively solitary, preferable to painful conversations with real people.

Unfortunately, this path takes me back to the university. It is not a place I wish to return to. I decide that if I have to go I should make the most of it. I call the English department and they agree to give me a copy of the videotape of the speech Dr. Pratt gave on the night he was murdered. I will research Pratt in the library and then bring him home with me for supper.

I have to decide whether to bring Judy along. It might be a long stretch in the stacks. But then again it could be a long stretch for her to be on the boat alone. When I ask her which she prefers, she is silent for a bit and then gives me a lesson in logic:

"Well, Jon, if I stay at ... at home, I am the whole day with my ... my own self. And if I go to the li ... library, I am with my own self, plus

48

… plus my brother of mine. It is like two … two scoops instead of one scoop. I think … I should say … I think I will take two scoops."

Unimpeachable.

We are barely out of the driveway when Judy starts singing. She has always liked to sing in the car. It is one of my first memories of her—me sitting on my mother's lap, my father driving, and Judy standing on the front seat in between, one hand on my mother's shoulder, the other on my father's, singing her heart out to Jesus.

"Jesus loves the little children, all the children of the world."

Actually, Judy sings pretty well. I noticed even as a kid that she never stuttered or started over when she sang. The words come out in a steady stream, like water from a hose. If she doesn't always hit the note, she's usually in the vicinity, close enough for friendly singing.

"Red and yellow, black and white, they are precious in his sight."

I guess someone is still singing this song. Friendliness is the whole point of singing for Judy. It's a way of showing that everything is all right. In this case, that *we* are all right.

"Jesus loves the little children of the world."

The words may have soothed me when I was a child, but they ring pretty hollow this time around. If he loves the children, why are so many of them hungry?

I don't join in.

But Judy has a creaturely persistence about her. She simply sings it again and then starts in on another.

"Rolled away, rolled away, rolled away. Every burden of my heart rolled away."

This one has hand motions. Judy, sly dog, knows I used to love the songs that had hand motions—"Deep and Wide," "I May Never March in the Infantry." Something about getting the body in sync with the spirit.

"Every sin had to go, 'neath the crimson flow …"

What are the chances Judy could explain to you or to herself what the "crimson flow" is—or what it means to be "'neath" it? It doesn't matter.

These songs aren't appeals to logic, and they roost somewhere other than in your head.

"Hallelujah! Every burden of my heart rolled away."

I have to admit that watching her circle her little fists around each other—in my memory of her as a little girl, and now in the car—makes me laugh. I give up and join in with her, and we roll away our burdens one more time.

By the time we get to the freeway, we have climbed up Sunshine Mountain, proclaimed our allegiance to the B-i-b-l-e, and hid ourselves in the Rock of Ages. Speeding along, we shout out "V is for Victory," and answer the question "Are we downhearted?" with a defiant "No! No! No!"

As we approach the exit for the university, you can't imagine two better-armed Christian soldiers than Judy and me. But as I park the car, I am back to anxious reality, skidding fast toward unmarked places on the map.

After thirty minutes in the library, I am cautiously optimistic. Not optimistic that I will find anything helpful for Mrs. Pratt, but that I won't lose myself or make a scene.

I have actually had some good experiences here in the past. It is, after all, a palace for books. A shrine to the mind and spirit and imagination. If the world was drowning you or boring you, here were tens of thousands more worlds. "The best which has been thought and said," some Victorian claimed. How could that be anything but encouraging? All here, under one roof.

But who's to say what's "best"? And "best" for what? Aye, there's the rub, matey. The powerful determine what's best, that's who, or so they taught me at the U—it's the bankers and priests and presidents (they didn't mention themselves, with their PhDs) and arms makers and media moguls and scout leaders and Sunday school teachers ... why hadn't I seen it growing up? It's the Sunday school teachers who strangle the world. It's Mr. Ring. It's Miss Sinclair.

So much information in one library, mountain ranges of information, Mariana Trenches of it. Earthly metaphors are insufficient; one has to go galactic to find adequate imagery for the near infinitude of what there is to know—even in this single word palace—and the heartbreaking finitude of my one little brain.

They say computers are going to help. The card catalogue has gone the way of the slide rule. The computer, the Internet—they will save us. They're charging over the hill, bugle blaring, chasing away the bad injuns of chaos and confusion. I have my doubts.

Pratt had a screed against typewriters as I recall, and said the same would be even more true of computers. Something about the imposition of the pseudo-order of mechanical regularity on the fecund anarchy of words—or something like that. Just another artificial layer between the buzzing, blooming world and our depiction of it in the written word.

Among the things I collect in the library are a graduate school catalogue and the English department newsletters for the last two years. Dr. Pratt is still alive in the catalogue, though six months underground in the putative world. Preserved by the inexorability of catalogue deadlines, his pixilated image stares confidently from the page, surrounded by the highly condensed detritus of his accomplishments: "Richard Pratt, Hamm's Professor of Contemporary Culture. BA Darlington College, MA and PhD University of Memphis. Specializing in literary theory, film, and Native American erotica." Then a list of awards, major books, and university honors, including Humanities Teacher of the Year not too long ago.

Out of curiosity, I glance at the course offerings, wondering if any of the old categories have survived in the decade since I shuffled away. I am glad to see that many have, though I notice the phrase "and Culture" has been added to most of the period titles: "Nineteenth-Century Fiction and Culture," "Readings in Medieval Literature and Culture." Seems innocuous enough. The tone, however, suggests alarm. Words like "hegemony" and "power" and "canon" float freely through the course descriptions. One gets the feeling that the past is out of sorts and needs to be set aright.

All this is interesting enough to a one-time foot soldier in the academic wars, but nothing here is of help for finding who killed the Hamm's Professor of Contemporary Culture. No listing in the index under "M" for murderer.

I turn to the English department newsletter. It is actually a fairly substantial publication that comes out three times a year, keeping everyone abreast of goings and comings, advances and retreats, kudos and backstabbings. I leaf through a few without profit, then notice that each issue has a "Recent Publications" page.

This is what I came for. What had Pratt been writing about of late? It couldn't hurt to know. I go to the most recent issue and don't find him listed. But in the next most recent, the issue in fact from last spring, around when he was murdered, I find the following: Richard Pratt, "Interrogating the Truth that Never Set Us Free: Toward a Deconstruction of the Literary Influence of the Bible and Other Sac(red) Texts," published in *Semiotics Today*.

I wonder whether it would be worth the effort to track it down. The article was published almost a year ago, probably written at least a year before that. Not much chance it will provide any insight to a homicide. On the other hand, it would justify my having come to the library, and be another hour of income for Judy and me. And to tell the truth, I'm curious to hear what Pratt has to say about the Bible.

Now the Bible and I go way back. My first memories of it are all positive. Everything after my parents died is appalling. I loved the stories; I hated the judgment. David and I slayed Goliath a thousand different times. Me and Moses and Cecil B. DeMille crossed and recrossed the Red Sea. I marched around Jericho until my legs fell off, watching for those walls to come tumbling down. And don't you know I loved the healings. "Pick up your bed and walk!" "Lazarus, come forth!" So cool. Facing down sickness and death on Main Street at high noon. Jesus was the new sheriff in town. Bad guys beware.

And then I discovered I was one of the bad guys. Sin to the left of me. Sin to the right of me. Sin all through me. I wasn't just a sinner; I was Sin Itself. God hated sin. Ergo, God hated me. I knew nothing about "ergo," of course, but I knew I was messed up. I knew I loved the darkness. I knew I faded away from myself for long stretches, and when I came back there was hell to pay.

And Uncle Lester was always going on about the Bible and what it said and how I was going to burn for what I did and what I thought. I had no trouble believing he was right. And I've had no trouble since then believing it is all foolishness. But back then I believed it was true in my bones. Now I believe it's nonsense in my head. And what's only in your head doesn't have a ghost of a chance against what's in your bones. So I want to see Pratt deconstruct it all again, in hopes of momentary relief from what ails me.

Of course, I am asking too much. Not that he doesn't have some good lines: "Many stories in the Bible carry within themselves a mirroring assertion and counter-assertion, leaving us with a beautiful symmetry of meaning negating meaning. Consider the story of the two thieves on the cross. Beckett, as usual, asks the right question. Does this story counsel hope or despair? 'One was saved; do not despair. One was lost; do not presume.' Three words balancing three words, followed by three canceling words balanced by three more canceling words. The story allows neither despair nor hope. It allows only a smile at the ability of language to affirm opposite realities at the same moment."

Not bad, but mildly disappointing. Not much thrill anymore. All stories, it seems, do the same thing. All boil down to the same residue of binary self-contradiction. Shocking once. Now, alas, just a bit boring. A bit too absolute.

I am about to close this issue of *Semiotics Today* and entomb it once more on the periodicals shelf, perhaps never again to be seen by human eyes, when I discover something very interesting. Following Pratt's piece is a response to it, written by one Daniel Abramson.

It is unusual for a respondent to an academic article to be from the same institution as the author. A coliseum full of academic gladiators would happily have crossed swords with Pratt, not least his fellow theorists. Why would the journal pick Abramson? Did he volunteer? Did

Pratt suggest it himself? More to the point, were there any waftings here that might be relevant to that letter opener in the heart?

One thing at least becomes clear in reading Abramson's response. He not only disagrees with Pratt on almost everything, he believes the ascendancy of Pratt's way of seeing the world signals the end of Western civilization and the beginning of a new Dark Ages. Sort of how some people felt when Captain Kangaroo went off the air.

Not that Abramson has any particular devotion to the Bible. But he is still a sucker for the idea of truth—that it is out there somewhere, that it can be tracked down, glimpsed from afar, snuck up on, maybe never quite captured, certainly never tamed, but also not a mirage, not something we make up, some comforting rag doll that we should put away when we're old enough to know better. "Truth," Abramson writes, "may be a chameleon, but it isn't a unicorn."

Abramson ends his piece with an unusually personal, even emotional, flourish: "I have lived under circumstances that make one believe in the categories of true and false, good and evil. Wiping away such categories serves oppressors and death. What many highly intelligent, but otherwise foolish, members of the academy seem not to realize is that their casual disembowelment of all useful notions of truth and meaning not only reveal them to be logically fatuous, it renders them irrelevant. When you start with some version of the assertion, 'There is no truth,' you have disqualified yourself from offering a second assertion. You have announced your own blankness and withdrawn from the struggle, and we rightfully conclude you have nothing to offer the rest of us as we try to understand how best to live."

Poor Daniel Abramson. Like his namesake, he lives in the lion's den, only these lions are not likely to keep their mouths shut. It's hard not to feel sorry for him. He had been a triceratops at the peak of his strength when a huge fireball streaked across the sky with the brightness of many suns, then disappeared far beyond the horizon, where a small flash appeared. Only slowly did the sky start to darken, never to brighten again. Only slowly did he realize this was not a darkness like other darknesses.

Abramson and his kind fell victim to the first law of evolution. Survival of the fittest does not refer primarily to strength but to reproduction. It's not the warriors who survive in the gene pool, it's the lovers. Abramson had an admirable view of the world, maybe even a noble one, but the people who held it with him hadn't reproduced themselves, at least not in great enough numbers. They are beyond being an endangered species. Their habitat has all but disappeared, and Nature, a remorseless mother, has rendered its verdict and bid them adieu. (A-dieu, go with God—and take God with you.)

I leave the library slightly more depressed than when I came in. I pick up the tape of Pratt's last talk in the English department office, sort of like stopping at the landmine store on the way home. Judy and I don't talk as we ride back to life on the waters. My old friends are back. I have ignored their presence for a few weeks, but now they're getting louder.

back for sure back for good back never to depart again

ELEVEN

I feel sick the rest of the week—all weakness and flight. I can tell Judy is worried about me. Normally she treats me with the benign superiority of a big sister. But when she is worried, she starts to hover. She especially doesn't like me going to bed in the daytime, no matter how lousy I feel.

Judy watches as I lie down on the couch for the third time in two days.

"I … I do not think, Jon, that you should be … I should say … that you should be sleeping so much. Sister Brigit says it … it is not good for you."

"Sister Brigit is way too anal."

Judy just looks at me with a few solemn blinks. I feel guilty, my default stance toward life.

"Listen, Jude. I don't feel well, see? It's that simple. When people feel crummy they lie down. It's not a crime against God or man or Sister Brigit. Do I have to accomplish something every lousy day of my lousy life? Can't I just be? Can't I sometimes buy a pound of hamburger with my good looks? Huh? Why become a worker ant serving the Queen Bee of Productivity? Jeez, Jude, I had a wife once. I don't need the spirit of Sister Brigit hanging over me. I just want to get up some morning and feel that the universe approves of me just for existing. Just for breathing in and out. You know, just how Margaret Mead reported those Pacific Islanders feel. Accepting life and themselves and sex. If you're hungry, just reach out for that mango hanging above your head. If you're

56

horny, just smile naturally at the next naturally good-looking girl that sarongs naturally by. Were they pulling her leg? Could it have been that easy—that guiltless? Why doesn't it ever work north of the equator? Is it the water? Is love—or anything else—ever really free? Will any woman anywhere ever be genuinely indifferent when she sees her lover making eyes at someone else? It's hard to believe, Jude. I mean it's really hard to believe. I've been asked to swallow whoppers all my life. First it was Bible whoppers—granddaddy creator, water turned to blood, chariots of fire, the dead come back to life. Then it was science whoppers—Big Bang plus time equals me. Out of dead matter … life! Out of chemicals … Consciousness! At least with the big Bible whoppers there was an equally big payoff—glory by and by, everything evened up and everybody happy … maybe the biggest whopper of them all. I mean everybody happy, Jude? No pain? No suffering? No stomachaches? You don't got to be no Sigmund I. M. Freud to see that's wishing more than thinking. But how am I any better off for not believing it? Why is that any more of a stretch than sea water plus lightning, bake for a few billion years, and you get the Sistine Chapel … or Michael Jordan going to the basket? Whoppers! Whoppers all around!"

I wind down like a Christmas toy on a dying battery.

"Are … are you finished, Jon?"

"Yes, I'm finished." It isn't pleasant doing improv performance art in front of an unappreciative audience of one.

"I just … just want to say, Jon, that Jesus … I should say, Jesus loves you … very much."

Great, that and five bucks will get me coffee at Starbucks.

I just said I'm sick for the rest of the week, but to tell the truth I've never been very good at measuring out time. Maybe it's been a week, maybe not. Time does not so much pass for me as it escapes—even hides. When I lived with Uncle Lester, I would finish breakfast and next thing I knew I'd hear them calling me to supper. I would be sure it was Thursday, only to find it was Saturday. I'd be listening to the first inning of the baseball game on the radio and next thing I knew the game had been over for an hour.

Maybe that's why I've had trouble making a living since I quit getting free meals in the army. If time is money, I'm a pauper on both counts. Zillah used to say I lost track of time on purpose. After another of my famous no-shows, she said, "If you think losing track of time gets you off the hook, Jon, you've got another think coming."

I didn't know exactly what she meant, but then I often didn't know what Zillah meant, or if she even meant to mean anything. She was just frustrated living with a psychological black hole.

In my own defense, I don't think I get enough credit for accomplishing simple things. Zillah never realized how much effort I expend just getting myself upright in the morning. If life is a race, I'm running in cement boots, but at least I'm doing the work. From a certain point of view, I'm even courageous.

But it takes more than a certain point of view to make a woman happy. I know how Zillah felt. I wasn't happy living with him either.

Maybe that's why I missed Judy so much over the years. When we were kids she could keep me patched together. She could do what all the king's horses and all the king's men couldn't. It wasn't what she said. She never said anything she hadn't heard someone else already say. It was just, I don't know, her presence—maybe with a capital P. She has a quality of being that is somehow soothing. Maybe she lacks the complexity necessary for sustained unhappiness. She is elemental in a compound world.

I remember the time not too long after we went to live with Uncle Lester. I'd gotten a whipping for something. I don't remember exactly what—with Uncle Lester most any excuse for a whipping would do. Apparently I sort of went off the deep end this time. I guess I cursed him and kicked him in the shins, but I can't say I remember it. (I wish I did.) What I remember is finding myself in the closet with Judy sitting next to me talking. I remember us sitting on shoes and dark winter coats hanging down around our heads, my face hot and wet with tears.

"It will be … I should say … it will be all right, Jon. He is gone. He will … he will not hit you any … anymore. I am here with you my own self. Are you hearing … I should say … hearing me, Jon? You … you come back now."

Judy was forever saying things were going to be all right. She never offered a shred of evidence to back up such an outrageous claim. She never gave reasons or arguments or precedents or anything—just bald assertion. Everything is going to be "all right." My God, what unsupportable optimism! All right? All right? Everything in its place? Everything as it should be? What could ever lead anyone in this wasteland of a world to come to that conclusion? Shantih my ass.

And yet, I don't know, there is something persuasive about Judy. You know she can't read, add numbers, dial the telephone, or quite comprehend a calendar. But you also feel she was born knowing things the rest of us never quite learn. She came into this world trailing clouds of glory, and, somehow, avoided the prison house of adult perception. She projects trustworthiness. If she can't calculate, she also cannot be calculating. She cannot strategize, maneuver, orchestrate, simulate, feign, invent, hedge, or dissemble. She is therefore totally unfit for this world, or most fit of all. All I know is that when I lost her the first time, I lost my best hope. I can't afford to lose her again.

TWELVE

After recovering a bit from my cosmic drift, I decide to show Judy I am a supernova of achievement. So I gather my courage like a hen gathers her chicks and suggest to her that I am going to review the videotape of Pratt's speech the night he was murdered. She just looks at me mournfully and goes up to her room, closing the door behind her.

I shrug and put the tape in the machine and turn on the television. Seeing Pratt talk on the night of his death is like watching the clip of Jack Ruby shooting Lee Harvey Oswald. Oswald has a little smirk on his face as he is escorted along the underground hallway by the sheriff. He seems to be enjoying the attention. He doesn't realize he's not the only killer in the crowd. Likewise, Pratt is animated and enjoying himself, displaying his wit like a young man showing off his flashy sports car. It never occurs to him, of course, that someone in the room may want him dead.

Pratt is dressed in a stylish cream-colored suit. His thinning brown hair sweeps from front to back in delicate waves. He smiles easily and often. His voice is calm, even soothing, and—no small irony—authoritative.

"It is indeed a pleasure to be with you tonight. I want to thank Dr. Cloud for her undeservedly warm introduction, and to thank the committee of the Dunkirk Prize for this equally undeserved award. And, of course, I want to thank you for bothering to show up. I don't know what you have come expecting, beyond the baked chicken, but I hope I disappoint that expectation—otherwise I will be as predictably dull as a political stump speech and you as predictably indifferent."

Pratt pauses for the polite laughter. A small man, he seems slightly overmatched by the large podium.

"Not, of course, that indifference is of necessity a lamentable state. Given the cultural forces of reaction in our society, the natural indifference of the great unwashed is, I sometimes think, our greatest defense. Even demagogues have difficulty rousing a hibernating bear.

"It is, in fact, about 'indifference' that I wish to speak tonight. Not about the single word, 'indifference,' but about the two words, 'in … difference.' The latter, of course, as Saussure long ago pointed out, is the key to all language, hence to everything.

"For what is language but difference, discriminations between similar but unlike sounds, and what are we but the product of our linguistic conceptions—the attempt to articulate ourselves against the void—and what is reality if it is not we?

"But of course this is an absurd assertion on my part. Who in our time can use the word 'reality'—singular or plural—with a straight face? For much of the twentieth century we thought speaking of multiple realities was quite radical enough, quite sufficient to give us the metaphysical scare we all crave.

"But now we know better. We know that we do not know. And if we are not happier, we are at least more playful. Play is now possible again in the West, as it has not been since Plato's poet-free Republic, since the Apostle's Creed, since Newton's laws and all other creeds, systems, explanations—in short, since all soul-quenching metanarratives tightened their fingers around our throats, choking off the life-giving breath of impulse, élan, and eroticism."

I have to smile. I had forgotten the swashbuckling quality of the contemporary academic theorist at the helm of his own rhetorical ship, sails billowing, cannons blazing.

But I also notice something I hadn't when I was there that night. The video cuts to the audience now and then, and the audience, alas, looks bored. The deconstructionist, the shape-changer, can work with any response—except a yawn. Heresy is exciting; ho-hum is death.

Dr. Pratt goes on.

"And no ideology, of course, has been more subtle and choking than the venerable doctrine of realism. Ah yes. Realism. The fascism of literature. It purports to cement the signifier directly to the signified. It seeks to naturalize the connection between word and object, erasing all independent inquiry in the mind of the reader. In its dictatorial zeal for unity, it tries to conceal the arbitrariness of the sign, to divert the reader's attention always forward down the road so that she does not notice the rhetorical bridges collapsing behind her.

"But those bridges are falling down, just as surely as the London Bridge of the nursery rhyme. For what is literature about if not its own failure? To what does language, rightly understood, testify if not to the death of language? Yes, Mr. Yeats, 'the centre cannot hold,' but it is not merely the center of Western culture that is not holding in your sentimental lament; it is Language itself that cannot hold—and therefore nothing can. Literature is not a testimony to successful communication between lonely creatures. It is the mausoleum of the Logos, the totalitarian word that would organize the universe."

(Ready the canons! Steady now, lads. Fire!)

"This is precisely what we see enacted in the poem that provides our text tonight. Consider Wordsworth's memorable line, 'Our birth is but a sleep and a forgetting.'"

Pratt goes on to disassemble one of the great poems of Romanticism. A familiar ritual. It is saying one thing, but no, it is saying the opposite. No, wait, it is not quite saying anything—an admission that, finally, there is nothing to say.

Or something like that. I am reminded how difficult it always was to follow Pratt all the way to the end of his pyrotechnic analyses. Each sentence usually made sense, and was winsomely expressed, but there was often just a tiny bit of logical slippage between one sentence and the next, until one was enveloped in a fog of assertions whose implausibility seemed irrelevant compared to its enchantment.

Pratt, of course, found a lot of sex in the poem.

"'Our birth is but a sleep and a forgetting,' says Wordsworth. 'Forgetting' is, one realizes, a buried reference to 'getting'—the great erotic impulse of life. It is the great engendering prong in the womb of the chaos. (I need not dwell, I am sure, on the significance three lines later of the word 'cometh.')"

Sex. Pratt's ability to find sex in the most unsuspected places was legendary. According to the lore around the department he once argued that "Mary had a little lamb" was the most pornographic poem in the English language, second in world literature only to the Song of Solomon. In a flattened, naturalistic world the orgasm (physical and ideological) is our only hope of rising above the tedious human condition. And when sex becomes tedious, what then?

Dr. Pratt has more to say, more immortal lines of poetry to disarmingly disarm. The fanfares of Wordsworth's great ode are shown, sadly for some, to be just a collection of kazoos.

"What do we have here then? A poem in which an affirmation of being dissolves into a lament for nonbeing. A realization of nullity that at the same time cannot shake the nostalgia for unity. We cannot of course have it both ways, and neither can the poem. It effectively cancels itself out."

As the actor president said, "There he goes again."

"And that of course is the source of its attractiveness. If it purported to give us some bit of wisdom, if it offered to us the petty emotion of a long-dead scribbler, how could we possibly care? Would Wordsworth not be just another Sunday school teacher, as he was to become all too soon anyway, and his poem another bit of dusty sacred text? Who could bear the tedium?

"But no. We are saved. The poem says nothing to us—without apology. And so we are free to let our own intellect, our own emotions, play without limits across the text, delighting ourselves with whatever we find or invent, tied to no system, no crushing 'explanation,' no dictatorial 'truth.'"

Ah, the eagerly awaited knockout blow.

"And reading is now just as impossible as writing. Writing used to be thought of, in the innocence of yesterday, as perhaps the highest and truest expression of self. Now, we see clearly that it is, rather, the death of self. To commit oneself to words is to commit suicide. It is to sacrifice the personal to the impersonal, the noumenal to the mechanical. What are letters on the page if not the infinitely interchangeable symbols of impersonality? As soon as you have created a text, it becomes the 'not you'—divorced, divided, irredeemably Other. The 'you' in the text disappears amidst the infinite play between signified and signifier in the mind of the community of readers.

"So do not go to *King Lear* to find Shakespeare; he is not there. Neither, for that matter, is Lear. Go there only to find Language, the god who will not die until we do, testifying brilliantly to its own glorious failure.

"And do not go to *The Divine Comedy* to discover the mind of Dante. Dante sleeps with the fathers and is beyond our knowing. Go instead to Oz. If *The Divine Comedy* is the paradigmatic work of the Middle Ages, then *The Wizard of Oz* is ours. Think for a moment—four characters in search of the Victorian virtues of courage, love, and wisdom in order to reach that most desirable of all destinations—home. And to whom do they look to provide them these things? The Wizard. And who is the Wizard but the writer—wise, powerful, intimidating, keeper of the flame, of the tribal secrets. And who must be killed in order to preserve courage, love, wisdom, and home? The Witch. And what is the Witch, of course, but all that frightens us: chaos, meaninglessness, our darkest desires—in short, the id."

A shadow of weariness passes over Pratt's face. He is building toward the big finish but starting to labor. A kind of sadness seems to be overtaking him. I had not seen this from a distance that night, but I can see it on the video.

"And so our fearful band kills the Witch with a ritual baptism of water and returns to the Wizard for their reward. But what do they find? The Wizard is a fake, just like our trickster writer. He is not Oz the Great and Powerful; he is the little man behind the curtain pulling the levers. And that curtain is the curtain of Language, and those levers the manipulations of style. And when the illusion is discovered, what does the Wizard-writer do? He tells our seekers that he has nothing to give them but a point of view, a way of looking at things. If you want courage, think yourself courageous, and, from one point of view, you will be. Likewise with love, and wisdom, and, yes, even home."

As I listen to Pratt, I, too, am trying to think myself courageous. But what I really want is a stiff drink, no ice. The dull ache in my stomach is increasingly less dull.

"This sleight-of-hand is the author's final trick before his abdication. When he can no longer be Oz the Great and Powerful, the Wizard-writer is free to leave, to fly off in her or his balloon to explore the stratosphere. This is as it should be. When we acknowledge that literature offers us neither wisdom, nor love, nor courage, nor home—our nostalgia for them notwithstanding—then we can allow the writer to float freely on the winds of Language, taking us everywhere and nowhere."

At this point one hears the commotion off camera. I am so caught up in Pratt's voice and vision that I have forgotten all about Verity Jackson. Here's where she started talking back to Pratt from one of the tables near the platform. She shouts something. Pratt's head doesn't move, but you can see his eyes looking off to the right. His smile freezes into a kind of Dick Nixon death's-head grin as he continues.

"There is, I must inform you, no meaningful difference between *The Divine Comedy* and *The Wizard of Oz*. Each ultimately deconstructs into an assertion of nonbeing—one the nonbeing of a mythological religious cosmology, the other an equally mythological economic conceit. The traditional reverence for Dante over Dorothy, or *Anna Karenina* over *Batman*, is testimony to our stubborn but sentimental belief in Wizards, in the significance of patterned words, in the illusion that the values they prop up are self-evident realities rather than the momentary ascendancy of a point of view. But nonbeing is nonbeing, no matter what the starting point. The death of 'das Ding an sich' is the death of all."

Again there is something unintelligible coming from the audience. Pratt begins talking faster and faster.

"I am here to say, then, that deconstructionism deconstructs. Saussure was wrong. There is no 'difference.' All seeming difference, all distinctions, all fine discriminations, all 'A is not non-A,' all structure, all systems, all explanations, all wisdom is illusion. Nonbeing is the ultimate democracy, enfolding everything into sameness—which is to say, death."

death a deer a female deer

The noise from off camera gets louder. I remember now that this is the point at which Verity Jackson stood up and Dr. Cloud and others came to her and cautiously escorted her away. I turn up the volume on the video so that Pratt's voice is blasting. I can make out just one phrase from whatever Verity Jackson is yelling. Over and over, it's something like, "if no truth, then no hope."

Pratt finishes, but without much conviction.

"And out of this death, the death of monolithic 'Truth,' we anticipate, irony of ironies, our freedom—the freedom of women from patriarchy, of people of color from racism, of the poor from capitalism, of writing from mimesis, and, underlying it all, of language from the delusion of meaning. It is in that spirit of freedom that I leave you tonight."

He pauses and some begin to applaud. Then he says, almost to himself, something I had not picked up at all that night.

"Yes. Forgive me. I have always made an awkward bow."

This last part is covered by the growing applause, applause that is respectful but a bit perfunctory. Ten years earlier, this talk would have seemed transgressive and chock full of frisson, to use two of Pratt's favorite words when I was a student. But the old fizz is starting to feel like fizzle. As people approach Pratt to shake his hand, he looks tired and maybe just a little bit desperate.

hes desperate all right and hes not the only one

THIRTEEN

I don't recall what I did after watching the video of Pratt's speech. I must have fallen asleep right there in front of the television because I find myself waking up very early the next morning on the floor. The weak dawn light oozes through the curtains like blood through gauze.

I look blankly at an empty bottle lying beside me, one of three, and reach up and click off the buzzing white snow on the television. The only thing that hurts worse than my back and hip is my head. I get up and struggle up the steep ladder to my room and fall into bed. My next contact with external reality, some hours later, is the phone ringing. It's Brianna Jones. She wants to talk.

I have to say, I feel pretty heroic for making myself get up so I can meet her in a couple of hours. I hope Judy is noticing. I am being purposeful as hell.

After showering and dressing I come down into the living room and find Judy sitting at attention in a chair—back straight, hands in lap, eyes staring straight ahead, tips of her shoes just touching the floor. She betrays no sign of engaging with her surroundings in any way. With anyone else I would have said she was thinking. But I don't know if that quite applies to Judy. I don't know that, absent external stimuli, she has an interior life. She certainly feels things, and she has a kind of intelligence, but does she think? Does she push ideas and possibilities around? Does she ruminate? Does she, like the rest of us, arrange and rearrange the data that comes in from this wolfish world, trying to hash out a livable compromise between what is and what she needs? Or is she simply content to be, a Zen master of extinguished desire?

Whether thinking or being, Judy doesn't seem thrilled to see me. She studies my face but says nothing. Clearly it is going to be up to me to serve up the first bit of conversation for the day. I try to sound upbeat.

"Well, Jude, what say you and I go out and see a slice of the world today?"

She doesn't answer. Not a good sign. Normally nothing gives Judy more pleasure than the ping-pong of standardized conversation.

"That was Brianna Jones on the phone. She wants to meet with us and have a talk."

Bingo. Judy's face brightens. Her eyebrows arch and she places her right index finger against her cheek.

"Well, that … I should say, that is interesting news, don't you … don't you think, Jon?"

"Very interesting, Judy."

"Yes, very … I should say, very interesting indeed."

When it comes time to go, I open the door and discover the first snow of the season lying mutely on the deck of the houseboat. Minnesotans love the first snow almost as much as they hate the last one. It changes things. Nothing seems the same as it was only a few hours earlier. The past is gone—and yard work with it—and all things become new. I could use a first snow for the soul.

Judy stands beside me staring out. Somewhere deep inside her brain the stimulus "snow" fires up the response "winter clothes." As a high priestess in the Religion of Order, she faithfully serves the goddess Routine. Routine demands the regularization of daily life into invariable rituals of small actions unencumbered by the procrastinating element of thought. The routines of life—dressing, eating, working, relaxing—give evidence that you and the world are on good terms. Everything has its place, every action its reaction.

For Judy the alarm clock is the initial call to worship. Alarm clock begets glasses which beget robe which beget slippers which beget toothbrush. The underwear drawer is followed by the pants drawer to be followed by the blouse drawer, leading, as night does to day, to the sock drawer and to the shoes in the closet. Were any of the drawers to prove empty, it is likely Judy would stand quietly staring until someone appeared to solve the mystery.

Judy's routines are often independent of external circumstances. In the past, ski hat, gloves, and scarves appeared on the first day of November, no matter the weather. November first, mild or menacing, began the winter dressing season. So it had always been, so it would always be, now and forever, amen. Maybe not literally forever; it had started with our mom and been reinforced by the nuns, but that was forever enough for Judy.

Judy looks at the snow then looks up at me, a bit reproachfully I think. She has come to live with a man who does not look at the calendar and has let herself be caught unawares.

"I have to get my ... my things."

I know I might as well sit down. Deflecting Judy from "bundling up" after November first is like telling the birds not to fly south. Instinct is Nature's trump card.

She drags out a large duffle bag that has been zipped up since the day she moved in. She draws out each item in order, like a priest laying out his vestments. I am stunned to see that the hat and scarf are the same she wore in sixth grade, knit by our mother.

First she puts on a brown cardigan sweater. Each button is a test. Her short, blocky fingers are not made for fine movement. Button passes into and through button hole only with the concentrated effort of a concert pianist. She buttons them all, then finds that she still has one button left at the bottom and nowhere for it to go. She stares at it for a moment, chin on her chest, and without a peep slowly undoes all the buttons and starts again.

After finishing she looks down at the row of neatly buttoned buttons descending her torso, rising slightly at the belly before dipping out of sight at the waist, and nods with satisfaction.

"There."

After the brown cardigan sweater comes the tan winter coat. The Scylla of buttons conquered, she faces with stoic calm the Charybdis of zippers. First she has to get the coat on. She always attacks the right sleeve first. Less an attack, really, than a negotiation. She pulls down the right-hand sleeve of her cardigan with her other hand, and then grabs the end of the sleeve with her fingers, a protection against the dreaded bunched-sweater-sleeve-in-the-jacket-arm.

Sweater sleeve in her right hand, she lifts the coat by the neck with her left, bringing the right armhole up to her face for a brief inspection before aiming her right fist, William Tell-like, for the dark opening. She always thrusts her fist upward, like a Black Power salute, raising the coat above her head. When her fist appears through the opening of the jacket sleeve she looks like Tommie Smith at the '68 Olympics.

If all this seems tedious, it is. Tedious to watch, tedious to describe, tedious to hear, tedious to do. But also a hedge against Seth, god of chaos, and a window into Judy's character, her nature. Therefore I continue.

Right sleeve conquered, but left sleeve still untamed. Right hand pulls down left sweater sleeve to be grasped by left-hand fingers. But now the left armhole cannot be seen. It is somewhere near the left shoulder blade. And because we are in the warmth of the houseboat, Judy is beginning to sweat. She must find the left armhole with nothing more than the memory of having done it before and the faith that she can do it again.

How does one both hold on to the sweater sleeve with the left-hand fingers and also use those fingers to probe behind one's back for an armhole that, because of the pivot of your right shoulder, moves away from you in direct proportion to your effort to move toward it? Such are the heartbreaking questions that life and winter coats ask of us all.

Judy chases the armhole in slow backward circles, like a dog chasing its tail. For some reason, it never occurs to me to help her, and she doesn't ask.

Eventually, the prodigal sleeve is found and the coat pulled on. Now comes the zipper, which fortunately is very large, with a handle like a small paddle. She brings the sliding part of the zipper down to the bottom and prepares to match up the two sides. No orbiting space capsules ever docked with more care than the two halves of Judy's zipper. Her chin again buried between her clavicles, she fixes her bulging eyes on the ends of the zipper.

Some days it takes the patience of Robert the Bruce to coax the zipper ends together, but this time she docks them on the first try. That done, Judy pulls the zipper up slowly, holding her jacket far out from her rounded belly so as not to snag the brown sweater. She doesn't stop until she has zippered past her neck to the very bottom of her chin. Stretching her neck like a chicken over the chopping block, she seals herself into her coat like leftovers in a ziplock bag.

But this still leaves too much exposed to the elements. Next comes the orange scarf that our mother knitted for her. It is too long, too wide, too loosely stitched, and therefore just right. Rather than throwing it behind her neck with the ends falling in equal lengths down her front, Judy holds one end against her neck with her left hand and begins wrapping herself, layer after layer, like a mummy. Her chin and mouth disappear under the last few turns.

Next comes the pathetic canned-pea-green knit hat. No self-respecting mongrel would be caught dead chewing on it, but Judy puts it on carefully, crowning herself like Napoleon at Notre Dame.

Hang with me. We're almost done.

Finally come the mittens. Blue vinyl with red and white piping, they fulfill the dream of American merchandising—the illusion of functionality and style with the minimum of quality or cost. The only real challenge is knowing which hand to put them on. Essentially flat and without differentiation from front to back, they looked like blue plastic flippers at the ends of Judy's brown puffy arms. And I forgot to mention the boots, which are in fact always the first thing she puts on. Now ready, Judy looks like a refugee from a bad 1950s space movie (redundant—they were all bad). Only nose and eyes remain exposed to the darts of life and weather.

She stands before me, a conqueror, fully prepared for the short walk to the car. I raise my right hand to her in salute.

"I am from earth. We come to your planet in peace and mean you no harm."

"Oh, Jon. Don't ... don't be silly."

We meet at a Dunn Bros coffee shop on Grand, near Macalester College. When Brianna Jones comes in the door, I am startled again by how beautiful she is. Tall, slim, erect, she carries herself like a Russian ballerina. She has a kind of dignity that we used to respect before we were taught to associate dignity with pretense and reserve with inhibition.

Judy sheds her survival suit, perfectly mirroring how she had earlier enclosed herself, and waves at Brianna like they are old sorority sisters. Brianna smiles and waves back. When she walks up to us she puts her hand out to Judy first.

"It's good to see you again, Judith. How have you been?"

"I have ... I should say ... I have been very, very well, Miss Brianna Jones. And ... and how about your own self?"

"As good as could be expected, Judith. Thank you."

"You are most ... most very welcome."

Then Brianna turns to me. I wish she hadn't. Beautiful women make me uncomfortable. Okay, even inanimate objects sometimes make me uncomfortable, but it's much worse with beautiful women. It's like they're a different order of creation, a separate species or something. There are men and there are women—and then there are beautiful women. You want to say they're just human beings like the rest of us, but it's not true. They may have the same allotment of internal organs, but they come from a different planet and live in a slightly altered space.

We sit around a small table. It's clear she's working hard to hold herself together. Undoubtedly she has given herself a "strong woman" pep talk on her way to our meeting. She projects a kind of controlled reasonableness that suggests she feels anything but controlled or reasonable.

"I asked to meet with you because I learned you're investigating Richard Pratt's murder. I want you to know something, but I don't want you to do anything about it."

This should be easy, I think. I am a master at doing nothing with the things I know.

"I mentioned to you when we met in the English department lounge that I was dropping out of the PhD program. They said they'd hold my fellowship for a year, but I won't be back. I only have to finish my dissertation, but I've decided against it. I'll never complete my degree."

She looks at me with an intense, defiant pride.

"But I wouldn't do anything differently. The last two years, up until last spring, have been the best of my life."

She gazes off into the distance.

" … the best I will ever have in my life."

I have a sinking feeling she is going to tell me why.

"No one knows this, but Richard and I were lovers. I hate how melodramatic that sounds, but there it is."

Judy smiles.

"Like Superman and … and Lois Lane."

Brianna tries to smile back.

"But I didn't come here to tell you about Richard and me. I asked to see you because I know who killed him, and I want you to know."

I widen my eyes and cock my head to indicate I'm ready.

"It was his wife. I'm sure of it."

"His wife? Mrs. Pratt?"

"Yes, his wife. She found out about us. It released a lot of rage in her, I'm sure, which in one sense would be completely justified. I am a woman. I don't blame her for her anger. It's just that she did not understand Richard and she could not have understood the relationship that Richard and I had. We were, I don't know, kindred spirits. You could even say we shared the *same* spirit."

I can tell she hates having to try to explain to me what she believes is beyond explanation.

"Do you understand how rare it is when your heart and your mind and your body all find simultaneous fulfillment in the same person? It's a coalescence that happens for one person in a million, and for that person only once in a lifetime. I had that with Richard for two years. I'll never have it again. I don't think that I even want it again. Not with someone other than him."

Yikes! What would Marlowe do? I resist the urge to tell her that the last word Pratt uttered as he died was her name. Instead, I try to sound logical.

"But Mrs. Pratt is the one who hired me to find out who killed her husband."

She looks disappointed in me, a look I am familiar with.

"Well of course."

"Of course?"

"What better way to divert suspicion?"

"Oh."

"She was desperate, Mr. Mote, desperate enough to stab him in the heart with his own letter opener. Richard was going to divorce her and marry me."

"Did she know that?"

"I don't know. She may have found out. She may just have suspected it. For that matter, Richard may have told her himself. He was a very honest man. He refused to dissemble or sneak around. He had assured me not even six weeks before his death that he was going to tell her soon."

"But even if she had wanted to kill him, Ms. Jones, she wasn't at the hotel that night. She never went to his talks. The police have established that she was at home the entire time."

Brianna looks suddenly exultant.

"That's just it! That's why I'm telling you these things I wouldn't willingly tell any other human being. Mrs. Pratt *was* at the hotel that night. I saw her with my own eyes."

I wait for details.

"The details aren't important. What's important is that I saw her. She was there, she lied to the police about it, and she had every reason to be enraged enough to kill him."

"Why haven't you told this to the police?"

Brianna looks pained.

"Mr. Mote, I don't know if you can understand this. What I shared with Richard was very special. I didn't want and—more than anything now—I *don't* want that dragged through the mud. And I have no bitterness toward Mrs. Pratt. She is a wounded sister, not a rival. It's not her fault that she was not Richard's equal. Few people were. Richard was a great man. He was speaking truth to power and he didn't deserve to die that way.

"If you go to the police now with what I've told you, I will absolutely deny every word of it. And I will sue you for defamation. But if the police try to pin this on Verity Jackson—or anyone else—I just want someone besides me to know the truth. I may be away and won't be able to tell them myself."

She pauses, then adds to herself, "far away."

away away far away you know all about away jonnie lets go away

FOURTEEN

On the way home from the meeting with Brianna Jones, my mind goes into rollercoaster mode, as it is wont to do when things get bad: it is all teeth-chattering speed, precipitous plunges, unannounced swerves to left and right, whiplashed accelerations—with no final, slowing entry into the station.

One of the tracks is Pratt. All would agree a good man. Gave generously to progressive causes, especially for abused women and disadvantaged people. A bit aggressive professionally, perhaps, but treated people well one-on-one. Went beyond the call to help students get jobs. Always courteous.

Polite and solicitous, yes. But something odd about being with him as well. What was it? He never quite looked at you. Looked past you, or over your head. You were in his presence, but he wasn't present to you. Know what I mean? Always seemed to be addressing you with only part of his mind—the rest was working on more interesting things.

It was like Pratt didn't think you were officially real. But no offense need be taken, because he didn't think himself real either. A favorite jag of his was on the artificiality of all things, including ourselves—"artificial" not being a bad thing to Pratt. First day of the first class I ever had with him, he says something like this:

"The root of the word 'artificial' is 'artifice'—a word that combines the idea of cleverness and deception with the notion of making and creativity. It's the Joycean, Daedelean word for the writer-inventor—'old artificer'—and it is a touchstone word for understanding the nature of things.

"All things, all facets of life, are artificial, because all things have been made—whether by the Big Bang or by Big Con(sciousness)."

He wrote it on the board, parentheses and all.

"You and I are complex configurations of rather simple organic compounds, the most complex arrangement of which is this thing called consciousness. A purely physical phenomenon, but much more interesting for that than all these tired-out, ghost-in-the-machine notions of the past.

"Human consciousness allows us to interface with the external world in exactly the same way that human touch or taste does. In fact, taste is an apt analogy for what you are doing when you interact with the world. Your brain 'tastes' the external world and reports its 'flavor.' Of course, the brain knows nothing of a truly external world. It knows only itself and its perceptions—its tastings.

"So who *are* you? The eternal question. You are, at most, a flavor, a taste at this moment and this moment only of an ever-changing configuration of atoms. You taste somewhat differently to yourself than to others, and no two people taste the same. But you are nothing more than a taste. There is no permanent you. No solid, stable, *imago Dei* you. Don't waste your time looking for it. Don't give your time and money to those who say they will help you find it. Instead, celebrate your protean evanescence. Be all things and no thing. Delight in being today what you never were yesterday and won't be tomorrow. Nothing else stays the same—why should you? All that is solid melts into the air. Savor the ecstasy of your melting."

All this in my first thirty minutes of knowing Richard Pratt. I remember being confused and thrilled at the same time. I couldn't explain exactly what he was talking about, but I knew I hadn't felt real for a long time, and he seemed to be saying that was okay.

And I didn't feel any more real three years later when I sat in his office and heard the bell tolling for my hopes for an academic career. Dr. Pratt was my dissertation director. It seemed a clever move on my part, given his stature in the field. I should have known that cleverness and I don't mix.

He warned me fairly early on that he wasn't happy with the direction the writing was going. Said it was theoretically naive—too much close reading of the text combined with mildly appreciative biographical connections and the random odd bit of insight. I tried revising chapters to better please him but to no avail. I just didn't have the proper theoretical squint. It came to a head in a Waterloo moment.

"I want to help you, Mr. Mote. I think you have potential. There's a place for you in the academy. But this dissertation, in its present form, won't help you find it. In fact, I personally could not approve these chapters as is. They have major problems."

I am a man acquainted with major problems.

"This approach may have been acceptable in 1955, but a lot has changed since 1955, including how we understand literature. You're writing about Melville as though it were Thomas Aquinas in that whaling boat instead of Queequeg. You're looking for little dried turds of truth in Melville when not even he believed in such a thing. Remember Ahab's coin? One text, many renderings."

I remember feeling more stunned than enlightened. My only response was a stammered question.

"Then why ... why do we read this stuff?"

"To witness the transgression of stultifying boundaries. And for the fun of it, Mr. Mote. For the play, the jouissance, the infinite potential, infinitely delighting, of playing with the text and allowing it to play with us. But to play with us, transgressive play. Not to inform us. Not, God forbid, to improve us. Not to palliate our sorrows."

I wanted to say that was too bad, because I had plenty of sorrows that needed palliating. Instead, I sat there knowing my life was making one of its characteristic sharp turns. I figured I could probably rework the whole thing in a way that Pratt would buy, but I also knew I wouldn't do it. It would have required a large amount of willpower and a fiery desire to work thereafter in a Pratt-shaped academic world. Willpower had never been my strong point, and jouissance just didn't seem like enough to live on.

I never blamed Pratt for my failure and I still don't. He just confirmed what I already knew: I was a poor excuse for a scholar, just as I was also proving at the time to be a poor excuse for a husband, and a brother, and now a detective, and everything else. Pratt was actually easy on me compared to Zillah, undoubtedly because she had more at stake.

Zillah accepted my graduate school flameout without a single "I told you so," but you could tell that she wasn't surprised. She knew before Pratt did that I wasn't living in the contemporary world.

I've become a firm believer that the sexes were never meant to live together. The Spartans had it right—keep the men and women separate and let them get together for a little R & R once in a while in order to make little Spartans. Pratt's whole spiel on everyone creating their own reality never looked truer than from inside my marriage. Zillah and I lived in parallel universes. Make that inverse universes. If she was yin, I wasn't yang—I was anti-yin. Our conversations went something like this:

Zillah: "Why do we never talk?"

Me: "We talk all the time."

Zillah: "I mean really talk."

Me: "What's this we're doing right now—macramé?"

Zillah: "I mean something more than 'Pass me the sports section' or 'What's on TV?'"

Me: "I'll talk about anything. Ask me a question."

Zillah: "I want you to ask the question for a change."

Me: "Ask about what?"

Zillah: "You should know what to ask about."

Me: "Okay, so here's the question, 'What the hell are we talking about?'"

Zillah: "We're talking about our lives. We're talking about the future of our marriage."

Me: "See. I told you we talk."

Talking. That's all they really want. It's as simple as that. Talk to them about things they care about and they'll stick with you through fire and flood. They'll work like slaves, raise your kids, and accept your potbelly.

But it's a higher price to pay than women understand. It really is. They think it's easy because they're born speaking the language. Men aren't, and it seems that just when you learn a few words, the language changes. It's like learning Russian so you can talk to your wife and then she switches to Chinese. You start talking to her on frequency band A and suddenly realize she's switched to band C. And she has more frequencies than a prima donna has whims. It drives you crazy.

But then pretty much everything drives me crazy of late. There's a kind of pressure building in my head and it's harder and harder to do even simple things. I find myself thinking about death quite a bit—mostly Pratt's death, of course, but there are other names on the list, including my father and mother.

Mom and Dad were gone before I really knew them. One windy night they got a sitter for us and went downtown for a rare celebration of something or other. Judy was thirteen and I was nine. We went to sleep that night safely ensconced in a typical American family, and we woke up as orphans. Some career drunk interpreted a red light as a challenge and accelerated through it into my mother's side of the old Mercury. She was extinguished immediately and my father fled into eternity after her a few hours later.

I remember very clearly having a dream that night, though you may smile and think it surely came later. In my dream, I was sleeping in my room. I woke up, and there were my mom and dad, holding hands at the side of my bed. I remember they were holding hands because I had never seen them do that before and I liked seeing it. And they had smiles on their faces, but also tears running down their cheeks. They seemed mostly happy in a sad kind of way. They didn't say anything, but just stood there and then waved goodbye, and my mother blew me a kiss and I started to blow a kiss back to her, and then they just sort of melted away and I woke up and knew I was an orphan.

Anyway, by the time we get home from seeing Brianna I am feeling as dark as I have felt in years. And the sight that awaits me doesn't help any. We park in the lot and unlock the gate that leads down to the boats. When Judy and I step onto the houseboat and then into the living room, my first impression is that we have been robbed. The place is unaccountably chaotic. I have known for a time that it is a mess, but somehow haven't really seen how bad things have become.

The condition of the place is a mute protest against any high view of human beings. The living room floor is strewn with newspapers and food-encrusted plates and dirty clothes. There are five or six empty beer bottles on top of the television. And I don't even like beer. There are blankets and a pillow on the sofa and one in the easy chair.

Upstairs, my bedroom has more sedimentary layers than the average archeological dig. You cannot identify the bed as such. It's covered with clothes and shoes and magazines. The lamp burns brightly without a shade. All the curtains on the boat are pulled closed.

Judy's room, on the other hand, is an oasis of order. Everything is meticulously in its place and at attention. The nuns taught her that cleanliness was a prerequisite for godliness. The behaviorists who took over for the nuns made it a prerequisite instead for a coveted can of pop at the end of the day.

A place for all things, all things in their place. Neatness is a cardinal virtue in Judy's cosmos. And because of this disposition toward life, Judy has an exponentially greater potential for happiness than I do. A made bed with hospital corners is a giant initial step toward a good day. Follow that with the expected breakfast in the expected order, the correct coat and hat put on in the correct way, the invariable day at the workshop putting the earplugs on the airline headsets, with the scheduled breaks at the scheduled times. Then continue with the normal rituals of returning home from work

heigh ho heigh ho

and of the evening, finishing off with the obligatory brushing of one's teeth. With so much in its correct place, there is little call for anxiety or ennui.

I have done Judy no favor by bringing her out of a world of ritualized contentment into one of random decay. She has been buoyed up by soothing order; now she has entered a precinct of the wasteland—tohubohu. It is like freeing your pet angelfish into the river above Niagara Falls. Freedom, yes, but to what end?

Standing in my post-Armageddon bedroom, I begin to lose my appetite for consciousness. It is my common response to stress. When the going gets tough, the tough get sleepy. Stubb had it right—"think not, and sleep when you can." Nothing can match the delicious feel of heavy slumber stealing into my mind, pushing away bills and voices and expectations and all that harasses me. I do not wish to die so much as I simply wish, for a while at least, not to be. Hamlet's choice seems an easy one.

Judy's aversion to my sleeping in the daytime is becoming downright mother-hennish. I tell her now that I'm tired out from the talk with Brianna and am going to lie down for a few minutes. She stares at me with that timeless look of disapproval that is hard-wired into women at the moment of conception. It makes me all the more anxious to close my eyes.

I go up to my room, shovel half of the debris off my bed, and lie down. But as I float toward oblivion, an ugly memory—an ugly face—floats up beside me. It is the face of Uncle Lester, the face as I saw it at my parents' funeral—the grim face of barbed-wire boundaries.

oh theres more to remember much much more

After the funeral the extended family returned to our house. "Extended" in our case meant only two sets of uncles and aunts—our father's older brother Uncle Lester and his wife Sherry, and my mother's sister Aunt Wanda and her husband Bruce. They called Judy and me into the living room. Uncle Lester did the talking, and he looked directly at me.

"Because of this tragedy which God has seen fit to visit on you, you are now going to have to depend on the kindness of others."

Maybe that was where God and I began parting company.

"Judy here is going to live with us, and you, Jon, are going to live with your Uncle Bruce and Aunt Wanda in South Dakota."

It hadn't even occurred to me that Judy and I wouldn't just keep living in our house. Some things slide right by a motherless and fatherless nine-year-old. I had lost so much so quickly that I was still staring down at my empty hands.

Judy began to moan. It started as a guttural vibration and built from there. Uncle Lester hadn't looked at her up to now, and he jerked his head toward her. The moan became a bellow and the bellow a wail. Aunt Wanda moved quickly to Judy and put her arm around her, but Judy was beyond comfort. Her lament carried up through the roof and out into the sky, the primal protest against that which should not be.

Judy's cry found an echo in my own soul. I didn't know why, but I too began to wail. Two bereft orphans in a world not arranged for their well-being. We were an inconsolable chorus of grief and fear and longing.

Uncle Bruce took my hand and brought me over to Judy, and Aunt Wanda held us both in her arms.

"We've made a mistake," she said. "We can't separate them. They've lost their mom and dad. They can't stand to lose each other."

Uncle Lester glanced at Uncle Bruce and saw that he agreed with his wife.

"The will leaves them to us."

He looked hard at Judy and then at me.

"We'll take them both."

We stayed another few weeks in our house. Uncle Lester had to deal with lawyers and insurance companies and other paperwork in the cities before we all went to their small house in Duluth.

The memory of that meeting in the living room, where our fate was decided in less time than it took Mengele to point left or right, accompanies me now into sleep, then withdraws to the bunker from which it emerged. But in its place come the voices.

send her away jon send her away or we will do it for you too much just too too much much much too much

FIFTEEN

I spend the next few days sitting on the deck of the houseboat watching the river go by. When I see a log float past I speculate that it is me. I want to go with it—on the river or in it are equally acceptable. When occasionally I am able to think consecutive thoughts, I chew on Brianna Jones's contention that Mrs. Pratt is the one who killed her husband. It causes a tightness in my brain.

One afternoon I'm feeling especially hemmed in. I ask Judy if she wants to go somewhere, just to get out for a while. Her face lights up like a searchlight.

"Well, Jon, how about … I should say … how about our very own Co … Como Zoo?"

When am I going to learn that even the most innocent question has the potential to reverse the magnetic poles? I mean, you ask if your spouse wants butter on her toast and the answer starts a pebble rolling that ends with you in divorce court agreeing to an avalanche of alimony payments. Do you think that Adam, when Eve started out for a walk in the Garden, asked in passing, "Would you bring me back something to eat? Maybe a bit of fruit?"

I don't want to go to Como Zoo because that takes us back into our old neighborhood again, and the last visit is still bubbling.

dont go dont go youll be sorry sorry sorry sorry

But, CEO of Confused Thinking that I am, I decide that familiarity and repetition might be the best way to exorcise the irrational fear that overcame me when we drove by the house before.

So we leave the dock and drive across the Wabasha Bridge and through downtown St. Paul, eventually hitting the freeway toward Minneapolis. It's a bright, mild November day. That first snow was a presentment of winter but not winter itself. Warmer weather has returned, and the real thing waits patiently high up in northern Canada.

Maybe because it's bright, I am feeling confident. Once we're back in Como, I even go a block or two out of my way to go past the old buildings where our father worked when we were kids. The place was Bethel College, and our father was their head maintenance man. Bethel was Baptist, which is enough to scare you right there. But they were Swedish Baptists, not Texas Baptists, so even though they thought you were going to hell if you didn't believe in Jesus, they at least felt bad about it. Not like Uncle Lester, who was grimly delighted with the idea that unbelievers were going to burn.

Actually, Uncle Lester hated the Bethel-type Baptists even more than he hated the "sexularists"—his term for the godless people ruining America with their immorality. In his view, libertines were "Romans being Romans," but diluted Baptists were traitors. He was proud to be a fundamentalist and thought self-proclaimed evangelicals were pretty far down the slippery slope to perdition themselves. I remember once trying to explain to Dr. Pratt the difference between fundamentalists and evangelicals, but he just waved his hand and said, "Evangelicals are just fundamentalists on Prozac."

Anyway, the Swedish Baptists eventually moved their college farther north to the suburbs, and now the place is a government job-training center. Once a place for training in the saving of souls, now a place for training in the making of money. Progress with a capital P.

The jewel of Como is the park. Lake, bandstand, sliding hills, walking and cross-country ski trails, golf course, kiddy rides, conservatory, and zoo. In the winter children race on the lake ice for speed-skating gold.

The youngest ones are encased in puffy snowsuits in a rainbow of colors, unprepared for the first overt competition of their competitive lives. They wait stiffly at the starting line on their trembling skates. The bang of the starting gun knocks two-thirds of them down. The rest run-waddle in little steps on the toes of their skates toward the finish line. Parents scream as though they've spotted Jesus descending from the clouds.

Judy raced here once, if you can call it that. She must have been eight or so. We had come to the lake to skate and found the races going on. All you had to do was sign up on the spot and you could enter. So Dad asked her if she wanted to race, and Judy said something about being the new Sonja Henie, and the next thing we knew she was at the starting line with her age bracket. There were only three other girls, but each looked intent on winning. The girl next to her was bent at the knee with left elbow raised, forearm parallel to the ice, her face decorated with an eyebrow-knitted scowl. Judy, on the other hand, was standing there waving at us like a red penguin.

The starting gun fired and the other girls, trying to start quickly, all fell down. Judy didn't react at all and was therefore the only one left standing. But rather than head down the ice, she reached over and tried to help the girl next to her get back up. The girl pushed her away and said something ugly. Judy looked up at us, put her hands palms up, and shrugged her shoulders. Dad and Mom were yelling for her to skate. The man who had fired the gun came over and pointed to the finish line and told Judy to get going.

So Judy started skate-walking down the ice like a drunken munchkin. When she was about halfway there the girl in the lane next to her finally got on her feet again and started skating after Judy. The other two were still struggling to get up.

Mom and Dad and I were screaming like crazy for Judy to go, go, go! The louder we yelled the more she waved at us as she took her mincing little steps toward the finish line. Unfortunately, the girl who had pushed her away was now taking long, ferocious strides down the ice. It was clear she would pass Judy right before the end.

That's when the miracle occurred. Just as the girl came up alongside Judy, she caught the toe of her long blade in the ice and went sprawling on her face. This time Judy kept going and crossed the line in glorious victory, me and my parents whooping and hollering and running out on the ice to congratulate her.

The other girl was crying and whining and made some comment about how people like Judy shouldn't even be in these races. Judy replied, with the calm air of a champion.

"Ne … next time p … p … I should say, pray to Jesus, and he will help you."

Jesus. Savior and protector of speed skaters. Who, for the moment, could doubt it?

There are a surprising number of people at the zoo for a November day. What is it that draws people to zoos anyway? Why do we enjoy exchanging bored looks with caged animals? You'd think we'd get our fill of that at the office. It doesn't even have to be some exotic animal that people have never seen before. It can be a lousy pocket gopher in its cutaway underground lair. You'd pay ten bucks to have it poisoned in your own yard, but put it in the zoo and we'll stare at it like it's the Shroud of Turin.

My theory is we're hoping to steal a little of their peace. Animals fit and they know it. They've got their job description down and they have no anxiety about how to fulfill it: "Eat things smaller than you. Run from things bigger than you. Negotiate with things your own size." What could be simpler? No "why am I here? What's it all mean? What are the others thinking about me?" Many's the day I would gladly trade places with that mangy buffalo over there. Him all hump and horns and cud, me all doubts and angst and stomach acid.

It's no contest. If we stare at it long enough, perhaps we can become as imperturbable as the moose.

One of Judy's favorites is the polar bear. So big, so white, with feet the size of catcher's mitts. You can watch him swim in his little pool from above and below the water. It seems way too small for him as he goes through his routine of pushing off from one side, coasting to the other, then diving down to the bottom on the way back to where he started. After the endless spaces of the open ocean, or the primal memory of them, he must be claustrophobic in this tiny tank and surrounding cement wasteland.

But maybe not. Maybe it's reassuring. Maybe the uncertainties of all that Arctic space were troubling to him. Maybe he likes knowing when he pushes off from one side that the other side isn't far away. I've pushed off before without any idea where the other side is, and believe me it's not pleasant.

"Well, broth ... brother of mine. Shall we go ... go see Ol' Mr. Ugly Face?"

This is Judy's name for the gorilla. She is normally laboriously respectful to all things great and small. But our dad had taught her to talk this way to the gorilla. He used to bring us to Como Zoo, back before they had the nice facility for the big primates, and would take Judy and me by the hand and walk up to the big silverback and verbally abuse it in a way that Judy thought was hilarious.

"So, Ol' Mr. Ugly Face, how are you today? Ugly as ever I see. And how is your ugly momma?"

Judy would double over with laughter and repeat word for word whatever insult our father had just offered the five hundred-pound colossus. The gorilla would just look back placidly, making things all the funnier.

We go to the gorilla house and Judy performs the routine. She finds it as amusing as the first time, but I can't get into it. Poor guy looks depressed, and I feel like we're kicking him when he's down. So I try a few lines telling him what a good guy he is and how I'm sure the lady gorillas really like him, and that he can be anything in life that he sets his heart on. It doesn't appear to help. He seems to want to be left alone, and so we oblige him.

As we leave the gorilla house, I see someone I recognize in the distance. It's Brianna Jones. She is walking rapidly across an open space by the now-empty summer seal pool and has a big smile on her face. I follow the direction of her gaze and see a young man striding toward her, also smiling. In a few seconds they meet and kiss. Then she takes his arm and they walk slowly away toward the big cats exhibit.

Brianna Jones? Martyr to ideological love, mourning her lost soul mate? Once in a lifetime? Apparently a lifetime isn't as long as it used to be. The postmodernist gods must be smiling on her to have provided a replacement so quickly. But I also can't help wondering if the lady hasn't protested just a tad too much.

SIXTEEN

All the way home from the zoo I play dodgeball with my thoughts. I am bothered by that kiss. There was nothing about it, or them walking off arm in arm, that looked like a new relationship. This was no rebound after recovering from the devastation of Pratt's death. It seemed like something that has been going on for a long time.

Of course, all this might just speak to the fickleness of women, and of Brianna Jones in particular, except for something else that flickers into my mind. I suddenly remember that when we talked at the coffee shop, she had passingly referred to Pratt being stabbed with his own letter opener. Detective Wilson said the police hadn't disclosed that detail. So how did she know it was a letter opener?

Maybe she knew because she was the one who had *used* the letter opener. Maybe she had discovered that Pratt had something going on with more than one "kindred spirit" and she couldn't live with that. People do kill their gods. I know I did.

Or maybe her zoo boyfriend had done it. Maybe he had found out about her affair with Pratt and killed him "in a jealous rage," as the tabloids say. Neither is likely, but there being life in the universe isn't likely either, yet here we are.

Seem, might, but, except, and a bunch of maybes. The story of my life. I need something more substantial. And so I decide to find out more about this boyfriend. It's time for some serious detective work. It's time for a stakeout. Judy will be thrilled.

The only way I can figure to identify the fellow is to find him with Brianna again and then follow him home or to work or to somewhere. Of course, I don't even know where Brianna lives or works. She's not in the phone book. But I do have her number from when we arranged to get together, and I know how to work backwards from a phone number to an address. So early one morning I bundle Judy into the car and we head for Dinkytown.

Brianna lives in a house there, just a few blocks from the university. I have no idea what her schedule is, but I figure she has to leave the house at some point, and that eventually she'll be linking up with mystery boy.

I take Judy with me because I can't have her sitting on the boat alone for days on end. Besides, like I said, I feel better with her around. A bit less scattered. Her simplicity is a kind of counterbalance to my multiplicity. When she's around I feel, I don't know, less haunted. Like Anaconda man and the little black boy.

Of course, I don't really know how to do a stakeout. On television they wait in vans stuffed with high-powered electronic surveillance gear. I have to be satisfied with sitting in an old Buick with my simplified sister, staring out the window at Brianna's front door a half block away. Judy brings along white powdered donuts.

I try to explain to her what we're up to.

"No, we're not actually here to see Brianna, Judy. Well, in a sense we do want to see her, but we don't want her to see us."

"Like … like hide-and-seek."

"Well, sort of. Except she isn't looking for us. We're looking for her, but the game is to have her not see us until we want her to."

"Like kick … kick … kick the can."

"Yeah, maybe more like kick the can."

"Where then, Jon, is … I should say … is home base?"

"Where indeed, Jude. Where indeed."

Stakeouts are low-effort, low-reward enterprises. We sit all morning without a single person coming or going from the house. I decide to leave a dozen times, but each time tell myself she might open the door just as we turn the corner, so we should wait five more minutes.

Somewhere shortly before noon I start to feel like I'm in a play with a bare stage and a scrawny tree.

Beckett again. Waiting for Godot—fruitless and endless waiting. My brain is awash with bits of novels and snips of poetry and flotsam of monologues and jetsam of Bible verses—all churning around with fragments of television commercials, sports trivia, and 1960s and '70s pop culture (1950s, even—reruns). Prospero, Zerubbable, drink to me only with thine eyes, tiny bubbles, Don Ho, Don Drysdale, Beany and Cecil, Cecil B., Mighty Counselor and Prince of Peace, good night sweet prince, I'd strike the sun if it insulted me. Ad infinitum, world without end, not with a bang but a whimper.

It used to drive Zillah crazy. She'd say, "What are you thinking?" and I'd say, "Those are pearls that were his eyes," and she'd say, "What the hell does that mean?" and I'd say, "Why this is hell, nor am I out of it," and she'd get up and walk out of the room. Who can blame her? I mean, at least the Pratts of the world get a salary for being pointlessly clever. I was casting my bread upon the waters for nothing, and nothing was what I got in return.

Anyway, I'm sitting there on the street outside Brianna's house all morning with Judy and it starts to snow. Unlike the first one, this is a snow that might stick around. Winter is coming to stay. It won't likely be bitterly cold for a few more weeks, but it's certain to be much, much colder before it will ever—if ever—be warm again.

cold cold cold tragically cold like the river

Just when we're about to leave, who drives up to the house from the other direction but Brianna Jones. Here Judy and I have dedicated ourselves to The Great Stakeout and she hasn't even been at home. Whether she left before we arrived or hasn't spent the night here at all, I don't know. I do know I have just wasted some more of Mrs. Pratt's money and have nothing to show for it. I decide we need lunch, a billable expense when engaged in heavy-duty detection.

It takes one more stint sitting outside Brianna Jones's house to deduce that she has a night job. An all-night job.

youre getting good buy yourself a deerstalker hat ha ha ha

So next time we show up at six in the evening instead of six in the morning, and sure enough, she hops in her car not long after and heads off. Turns out she works at a shelter for battered women. Checks in the women staying there, deflects the occasional angry boyfriend, plays with the kids who tag along, and generally makes the world—briefly, for a few women—a slightly better place.

I figure out she works eight to eight, leaving the shelter just after overseeing breakfast. The rest of the morning is her free time, before going home to go to bed. If she's going to see her boyfriend, it's likely to be between eight and noon.

So we begin staking out the shelter starting a bit before eight and get lucky the third morning. She drives around running errands for a couple of hours, then goes to the Hungry Mind bookstore on Grand about eleven. I am tempted to go into the bookstore after her. I could keep an eye on her, and if she sees me it would be natural to pretend to be surprised to see her there. But I can't trust Judy to pretend anything. She is liable to say, "My brother, I should say, my brother of mine has been following you."

About fifteen minutes later Brianna comes out and stands in front of the bookstore, looking at her watch and up and down the street. This is hopeful.

A couple of minutes after that, Judy says, "I think Mr. ... Mr. Romeo is here."

Sure enough, there's the guy. I am surprised Judy has spotted him. I hadn't thought she had seen him and Brianna at the zoo. Judy is taking in more than I realize.

Brianna sees him and smiles. When he walks up, they kiss again, just like before. Then they go into the little café right next to the Hungry Mind. Luckily for me, they're seated at the table by the picture window that faces the street.

Brianna never looks at her menu. She is talking intently, leaning forward and staring directly into his face, like women do when they want men to engage with them. ("Look into my eyes, you are growing relational, very relational.")

He has his menu open and is pretending to look at it, but you can tell his eyes aren't focusing. He looks agitated. The more she talks, the more he fidgets. Finally he puts the menu down, leans forward, and answers her. He gestures with his hands and shrugs his shoulders. She isn't buying it. She speaks again, this time tapping the table with her index finger, drilling her point home.

Then the waitress shows up and they order. The food comes quickly—salad for her, soup for him. They don't talk much more and finish in less than fifteen minutes. Brianna starts up again when the check comes. She looks to be instructing him. He is listening but not responding. When they come out onto the street, she grabs him by the shoulders, looks into his eyes, and says one more thing. He nods. She hugs him and they walk away in opposite directions.

Judy pronounces her blessing.

"He is a ... a very nice man. Brianna ... Brianna Jones likes him very, very much."

I watch him get into his car a block away. I pull out and follow him as he turns north on Snelling and then heads west on 94. Minutes later he exits into downtown Minneapolis, passing by the Metrodome. It seems likely he is headed back to work. If I find out where he works, it shouldn't be too hard to find out who he is. I just hope he doesn't disappear into the IDS or some other giant office tower.

But he doesn't drive to any office tower. He goes to city hall. He pulls into a parking lot across the street. I slip into an open spot on the street within sight of him.

Judy recognizes the place.

"This is where your ... your friend De ... Detective Wilson works."

"Yes, my good buddy the detective does work here."

"He ... he likes you."

"Yes, Judy. He thinks I'm the greatest."

"I think you are ... the greatest, too, Jon."

"Thanks, Jude."

"You are very welcomed."

I get out of the car and tell Judy not to move a muscle until I'm back. She salutes and stiffens herself into a statue. I watch the boyfriend cross the street and go into city hall. I go in after him and follow him through the giant building until he turns into the police department, then go back to the car, reviewing what has just taken place.

The boyfriend meets Brianna. She gives him a pep talk to do something he doesn't want to do. He drives to city hall and goes to the police department. To ... what? Confess? Inform? Renew his driver's license?

why does it matter why why why why

SEVENTEEN

Late one morning the next week I'm on the dock outside the houseboat, and a neighbor from a boat down the way walks by.

"Happy Thanksgiving, Jon."

Damn. How did I not know it was Thanksgiving? Then again, how did I not know a lot of things that everybody else seems to know?

this is only a test jon it is not your real life when your real life begins you will be given clearer instructions

Thanksgiving was a big deal when we were kids, almost as big as Christmas. Our parents always had a lot of people over, including students from the college who lived too far away to make it home. Uncle Lester and Aunt Sherry never came from Duluth. They always said they were busy with church responsibilities, but we knew it was because we played cards and engaged in other dubious activities.

Judy was a hell of a potato peeler at Thanksgiving. People like her aren't known for manual dexterity, but potato peeling is more about perseverance than dexterity, and perseverance is one of Judy's defining attributes. First thing in the morning on Thanksgiving Day, our mother would place Judy at the kitchen table with an Augean pile of potatoes in front of her, and Judy would set to work while Mom got the turkey ready for the oven.

can you spell rumpelstiltskin

And then an elaborate ceremony would take place as the Thanksgiving dinner was served. I remember our last Thanksgiving together.

After we had all sat down at the table, our father quieted everyone and said, "Ladies and gentlemen. The Lord has been very good to us again this year. He has preserved our lives, forgiven our sins, invited us to be members of his kingdom, and given us what we need to live. And for that we give him thanks."

He paused while everyone nodded in agreement, then continued.

"Moreover, this year, as in years past, he has further blessed us by allowing us to have our Thanksgiving meal prepared by two of the great chefs of the Western world. Please join me in showing our appreciation for chef Alice and chef Judy." At which point our mother came in holding high the huge brown turkey on our best platter, followed by Judy, beaming like she'd just won the Nobel Prize for Potato Peeling, carrying a giant bowl of steaming mashed potatoes. We enveloped them in applause.

So much love, so much food, so much fellowship. So much that was simple and right with the world. So much lost so quickly. I could weep about it even now. The next Thanksgiving we were at Uncle Lester's. Same day on the calendar, same food, similar words of gratefulness, but worlds away in every way that counted.

And now I find that it's Thanksgiving Day and I am like the virgins caught without any oil. I walk the plank back up to the houseboat.

ha ha walk the plank we like it we like it you aint seen nothing yet
and there stands a forlorn-looking Judy. She asks me a question that brings me to tears.

"Do we have no potatoes, my … my brother of mine?"

Yes, Jude, we have no potatoes. We also have no turkey. We have no stuffing, no cranberries, no rolls, no pickles, no corn bread, no gravy, no celery sticks, no Jell-O salad, no carrot salad, no lettuce salad, no butter, no milk, no pecan pie, no pumpkin pie, no apple pie, no transparent pie, no ice cream, no whipped cream, no cloth napkins, no pewter water glasses, no special tablecloth, no hand-crafted Pilgrims for the centerpiece.

And we also have no friends to invite over. No family. No one to tell stories about or to. No one to carve the turkey that we do not have. No one to recite the formula prayer. No one to say, "Let's join hands." No teenager to complain about having to join hands. Or to point out that the Pilgrims were really imperialists when you come down to it.

It's just me and you, Jude. Two daft ones putting our daft heads together against the winter winds.

I decide I've got to give Judy a Thanksgiving. The cupboards are bare in the galley and the grocery stores are all closed. But there must be restaurants open somewhere. Someone in America will sell you a turkey dinner at any time on any day if you have the cash. So I tell Judy to put on her best dress because we are going out for Thanksgiving dinner.

She brightens up and disappears up the ladder. I go and put on my good pants, almost-clean Dockers, and my only sport coat. I own no ties on principle, but I do have a white shirt. I look at my white socks and figure no one will notice, but then, inexplicably, I ask myself what Sister Brigit would do, and I scrounge out some black socks instead.

Judy comes out in a red dress. It looks battered to me, but she associates red with dressing up, and I'm the last person to argue. It's almost noon by the time we have assembled ourselves. We head for the car and then for the city.

We try Mickey's Diner first, surely a place that you could get turkey on Thanksgiving, probably even meatloaf, but it's closed. So are the next two places I think of. So I shift from purposeful to wandering, and we drive around for a while just hoping to find something. I start making vows ("We are not going to a McDonalds, I don't care if we run out of gas first"—which I then notice we are about to do). Then I start making threats, to the universe in general ("I've had it") and to God in particular ("Would it be so hard, Mr. God Up in the Sky Guy, for you to help us find one freakin' place for us have a freakin' turkey dinner so we could freakin' show you our freakin' thankfulness, thank you very much?")

Not long after which I spot a neon sign and a line of people.

"Union Gospel Mission" the neon light says. And on the window a big hand-scrawled sign, "Thanksgiving Dinner. Free. All Welcomed."

I'm not too proud. Okay, maybe I am, but I'm also almost out of gas and I have a woman in a red dress with me who is expecting a turkey dinner. So I say, "Here we are, Jude," like I'd planned this all along.

"Yes, Jon. Here we mo ... most certainly are."

By the time I park the car, the doors have opened and there's no line outside anymore. Judy and I walk inside and take it all in. Some people are already eating at long tables. There are old men and young men and middle-aged women—both alone and in small groups. There are families with young kids, some kids holding on tightly to their mothers' hands and some chasing each other up the walls and across the ceiling. Some people are dressed rough, as though they are well acquainted with the street, and others are dressed better than Judy and me. They are the colors of the United Nations.

And they are loud. They are loud because they are talking in all directions, and because many are laughing, and others are calling to people they see who they know further up in line or at the tables. But it is not an oppressive loud; it is a comforting loud, like our home used to get on Thanksgiving back when we were kids. Like when the noise is the good noise of people living and feeling happy, at that moment at least, with where they are and who they're with. Oh God, send us such loudness.

And while we are standing there, someone greets us.

"Welcome, happy Thanksgiving! Would you like to have dinner with us today?"

Judy answers because I am too emotional to say anything.

"Why, yes. Yes we would be very happy to have Thanks ... I should say, Thanksgiving dinner with you today."

"Well that's good because we have lots of food. And may I add that I like your red dress?"

"Yes, you may. I ... I like it very much my own self."

And so we get in line and then find a place at a table, me sitting between an old white man with gray stubble and huge hands on one side, and a young black woman with two kids on the other. And Judy sitting across from me, smiling at everyone and at me.

EIGHTEEN

Okay, so we have added to the list of suspects, like a good crime story should. Dr. Pratt has been murdered. Mrs. Pratt thinks Professor Abramson perhaps did it. Brianna thinks Mrs. Pratt for sure did it. It looks possible, at least, that Brianna or her boyfriend did it. (If there were a butler around, I would accuse him of doing it, but this story ain't got no butlers.)

how about your sidekick maybe she did it maybe shes a killer maybe shes more dangerous than you think maybe shes the one that needs to go we can help with that we can we can

And then there's Verity Jackson. What would Lord Peter do?

A feast for a real detective, but just hardtack and water for me. I'm supposed to be honing in on a killer. Instead I am proliferating possibilities. Give me a little more time and I could work out a plausible scenario in which the pope did it. Pratt was right, reality multiplies itself like rabbits. Stick with one unquestionable rendering of the world and you'll be fine. Allow the possibility of "on the other hand," and you have introduced a second rabbit. Soon you have four rabbits, then sixteen, and next thing you know there are more rabbit realities than can fit into one universe. So of course you posit a second universe, and, well, you can see where it goes from there.

While I am following Brianna Jones around and pursuing these rabbit trails, I make some other remarkably decisive decisions, like a goddamned General Patton. They are driven not by my getting better but because I am getting worse. Judy has suffered enough because of me—both because of my own self, as she would put it, and my … not my own self. Like John the Baptist, one of me is becoming less and less so that the other—others?—can become more and more. And they seem to be getting nastier. Most alarming of all, they're bringing Judy into it.

So I do three proactive things. I call New Directions (Judy and I still call the place Good Shepherd, even though it makes them mad) and tell them Judy needs to move back as soon as possible. They say there's a lot of paperwork to fill out and their admissions committee will have to decide. Space is tight, and I will have to certify her condition as with any new applicant. Certify her condition? She'd been there almost thirty years, counting the time with the nuns. They should have a good handle on her condition by now. But you don't want to rile petty bureaucrats. They can stop the forward progress of your life with paper clips, and they know it. So I sweetly ask them to send the forms.

Then I arrange to meet with Mrs. Pratt to give her an update on everything I don't know, which is almost infinite.

But before that, I need to meet with Brianna Jones. I want to warn her that I feel obligated to tell Mrs. Pratt about Brianna's boyfriend and his going to the police station, for whatever reason. It might be the only bit of new information Mrs. Pratt gets from me for all her investment. If the boyfriend went to the police to confess, she'll find out about it eventually. But I like the idea of Detective Wilson telling her, only to have her reply that I had already informed her of that fact. Put that in your pipe, Inspector Japp!

Brianna agrees to meet me at W.A. Frost on Selby—the Fitzgeralds' old haunt—after her all-night shift at the women's shelter nearby. I hope the spirits of Scott and Zelda are around to help. They certainly understood tag-team demons.

I'm sitting by the copper fireplace rehearsing my lines, staring at a painting of sheep huddling together in a blizzard while Judy blows bubbles into a root beer float. I think Sister Brigit would likely protest her ordering a float in the morning, but I find myself wanting to make her happy any way I can in the short time we have left together. I want Judy, if no one else, to remember me fondly.

As we wait, I review the night of the murder in my head and start thinking about what I was doing myself before and after Dr. Pratt's speech. I remember spending time among the book tables in the late afternoon. And the dinner and the speech. To tell the truth, I can't recall much about what I did after the speech. Seems like I had a few drinks at the hotel bar and then probably took my empty self to my empty home and went to sleep in my empty bed. Judy moved in a few days later.

While I'm sifting through the past, Brianna comes in looking beautifully wasted, if you know what I mean. Not beautiful *and* wasted, but beautifully wasted. Her eyes are sunken. You can see that spending nights sheltering broken women—*other* broken women I almost said—isn't allowing her enough sleep. Her black hair is stringy and her skin, while whiter than ever, has lost its luster. I think of Poe.

Still, she offers us a tired smile, and I find myself understanding why she may have meant more to Pratt than any of the others. And why he might have taken chances for her.

She and Judy exchange ritual pleasantries, and she orders hot tea while I look for a perky way of accusing her of complicity in murder. She leads.

"So, how has your research been going, Mr. Mote?"

I decide to be evasive, one of my strengths.

"Okay, I guess. No great discoveries."

"Or great suspects?"

"Not really. I've learned mostly what people already knew."

"Such as?"

"Oh, that there are significant ideological divides in university English departments, for instance. Bigger even than I knew when I was at the university."

"You're right, that isn't a new discovery."

"Did Dr. Pratt have any, well, enemies there?"

"No one who would kill him."

"Well, how about anybody who might want to at least give him a black eye?"

"Okay, he and Dr. Smith-Corona hadn't been on the best of terms lately. She wasn't happy about this and that, and it irritated Richard because he had hired her in the first place to strengthen the offerings in feminist literature, *after*, by the way, Women's Studies at the U had turned her down for a position. Richard felt she owed her career to him and he didn't like her complaining. I didn't think that was fair, but it's how he felt. But all that was just the usual in-house academic head butting."

She sits quietly. I ponder whether to disturb the universe. While working up my courage, I feint to a secondary topic.

"What about Professor Abramson?"

"What about him?"

I decide to be tricky.

"Well, Mrs. Pratt has told me."

How's that for a poker bluff?

"Oh. Yes. She *would* know about Professor Abramson, wouldn't she?"

I hold my fire, hoping for more, and am not disappointed.

"Only a few people at the university knew about Professor Abramson, and they were administrators. Richard was very careful to keep it from the other members of the department—for Professor Abramson's sake."

I nod. Keep *what* from them? She isn't just referring to ideological differences.

She takes a sip of tea. A wave of deeper sadness passes over her face. She is clearly troubled.

"I'm not proud of this. It was the only thing Richard and I ever fought about."

She is silent again. Judy stops blowing bubbles in her root beer and looks at Brianna, but doesn't say anything.

"Professor Abramson told Richard in a very formal letter that he had these early signs of this … this 'family disease' as he called it. Said it was possible that he might have to retire sooner than he expected, perhaps within two or three years. He said he wanted Richard, as chair of the department, to know this so that he could do some long-range planning for a possible replacement."

very professional."

"Yes, and very considerate. Professor Abramson is a gentleman, even if he isn't … I don't know … progressive."

Ah, yes. Progress. A wonderful concept.

"So Richard went to him and expressed his concern, which was very genuine. He always wished Professor Abramson well, even when they disagreed, which wasn't as often as people think. Anyway, after some questions Professor Abramson revealed the nature of the disability—the short aphasic spells, some memory loss, occasional disorientation. Richard told me he wasn't totally shocked. He had seen the signs himself."

Surprising news to me, but nothing so far to make Abramson murderous.

"And that's how things stood for a couple of months."

Brianna appears to be looking for a way to wrap it up there, but I know she can't. Some rocks, once they start rolling down the hill, don't stop until they've reached the bottom. I give a little nudge.

"For a couple of months?"

"Well, something like that. One day Richard just starts talking to the air, even though I'm with him. He says, 'You know, it's not fair to Dr. Abramson to allow him to slip into senility while everyone is around watching.' I say it's not senility he's dealing with, but Richard just keeps going, as though he doesn't hear me. 'He's had such a distinguished career, and has always carried himself with such dignity and grace, I know he wouldn't want to embarrass himself in front of all of us who respect him so much.' And I ask him what is he proposing be done. And he says, 'The worst part is that he won't even know he is embarrassing himself because his mental failure will at the same time diminish his self-awareness.'"

I feel a little sick. It sounds too much like what Dr. Pratt did with Tolstoy and Dante.

"And the upshot is that Richard decided that Professor Abramson, for his own good, should take early retirement, immediately."

"How did Abramson take to the idea?"

"He didn't—at all. But Richard had already gone to the provost and made the case. And the provost had agreed. Since Professor Abramson's growing disability could reasonably undermine his competence to do this job, the university was on firm legal ground to terminate his employment. And since Professor Abramson was not that far from retirement age anyway, the university could offer him an early retirement package with full benefits. It was really very generous. Richard insisted on that."

"But I take it Abramson didn't agree."

"No, he didn't. And neither did I. I told Richard that Professor Abramson deserved to choose the time and manner of his retirement. Richard said that was exactly what was not possible, because Abramson's disability had taken away his power to make such choices. He said it wasn't fair to students either. How could the department in good conscience continue to assign classes to a man who would be increasingly unable to teach them well? Or allow him to direct dissertations that could take years to complete?

"I said I didn't think he was anywhere near that debilitated and there was no proof yet that he would get worse. And then Richard said something that really stunned me."

She rubbed her temple with her right middle finger.

"He said, 'You realize, Brianna, that if there were a sudden opening next year, there's a good chance I could hire you as a temporary replacement. And then if you finished your dissertation at the same time, you'd have a decent chance of winning the position permanently. I could help make that happen for you.'

"He said it so tenderly, like he was proposing to me or something. I was speechless. I felt like he had punched me in the stomach."

So Pratt had pushed Abramson out. My God, Abramson *did* have a motive. And he was at the hotel that night. Killing Pratt would have been totally out of character, but it would not have been completely irrational.

no not irrational detective boy thats our job and we want to get on with it on with it on with it

All three of us sit in silence for a moment. Judy has finished her float and is twisting the straw into knots. I am trying to digest what Brianna has just told me and at the same time figure out a way to move to the original topic for the meeting.

"I can see why that would be hard, Brianna. It's not a good position to be in. I … well, I hope what I have to tell you right now won't be even harder. I have some other things I need to ask you about."

She looks me in the eye.

"Number one?"

"Well, how did you know Dr. Pratt was killed with his letter opener? The police never let that out, and last time we were together you said Mrs. Pratt was desperate enough to have stabbed him with his letter opener."

Brianna just stares at me for a moment.

"And question number two?"

"Well, this is a bit awkward."

"Awkward doesn't even begin to describe what all this is, Mr. Mote."

"You're right. Okay, the second question has to do with your boyfriend. I mean, who is he and when did he become your boyfriend, and why … well, why did he go to the police station a few days ago?"

Brianna sits up straight and folds her hands together on the table. I figure I've been busted, but I have a foolish need to explain.

"I apologize for having followed you around. I really do. But I just accidentally saw you kissing him when Judy and I were at the zoo and I decided it was my duty to Mrs. Pratt—and maybe to Dr. Pratt—to find out who he was and whether he might, by any stretch, have anything to do with … anything."

Brianna looks wearily amused.

"Don't apologize, Mr. Mote. I know you were following me. I saw you twice, once with Judy.

Judy takes that as a cue.

"We were playing … I should say … playing hide-and-seek with you, Bri … Brianna."

"I know, Judy. It was fun. Olly, olly, oxen free."

Judy smiles broadly.

"To answer your first question, Mr. Mote, I knew Richard was stabbed by his own letter opener because my boyfriend told me so."

Now it's my turn to be stunned. Maybe I've solved this whole thing after all!

"And to answer your second question, I've known my boyfriend since I was three, because my boyfriend, as you call him, is actually my younger brother. As for the kisses, we are a close family. We all kiss when we meet."

I try to look unfazed by yet another poke in the eye by my good buddy Life. I even try to move on with a question.

"The police station?"

"He works there. In the homicide division. He's a lab technician. I asked him to give me information. He resisted. Said he could get in trouble. Fired, even charged with a crime. I said I only wanted him to keep his eyes and ears open. He didn't have to rifle any desks or do anything dangerous. He didn't learn much, but it wasn't hard to find out about the letter opener.

"As long as I'm doing your job for you, Mr. Mote, I'll tell you one more thing I learned from my brother. Richard didn't die from being stabbed. There was a stab wound, but it was superficial. He died from the fall. He was stabbed and then pushed off the balcony. And you know who I believe did it."

So boyfriend is actually brother. Ah, sweet haplessness. I embrace you like a nursing mother embraces her babe. Yea, though I walk through the valley of the shadow of death, cluelessness goes with me.

death is our shepherd we shall not want

"Anything else, Mr. Mote?"

Why stop now?

"You said before that you saw Mrs. Pratt at the hotel the night Dr. Pratt was killed and that the details weren't important. I'm thinking maybe they *are* important."

"All right. I stayed behind at the hotel after the dinner. I wanted to be with Richard. I was proud of him for winning that prize. Almost no one knows this, but Richard had been struggling for quite a while with the

DEATH COMES FOR THE DECONSTRUCTIONIST

direction of his career. He felt the discipline was moving away from him. He had thought he was going to get some prestigious job offers from back east that never materialized. So getting the prize was a confirmation, you might say, of all that he had worked for. And I wanted to share that moment with him."

Sounds to me like a lifetime achievement award for an aging actor at the Oscars. The problem with being avant-garde is that avant-garde has a short shelf life. Picasso once outraged the Royal Academy. Now cheap Blue Period prints hang in dentists' offices. You can only play for so long. Eventually recess is over.

"So I decided to surprise him. I waited for an hour or so after the dinner—in case he had drinks with colleagues or something—and then went to his room."

"Was he there?"

(By which I really mean, "Was he alive?")

"Yes, he was there. But he wasn't himself. He was agitated. He said he was glad to see me but that he really needed to be alone that night. I asked why, but he just said he had some things he had to do and that he needed to be alone. Something was wrong, but I didn't know what. I was hurt, of course, but I understood Richard and knew he hated scenes, so I left almost immediately."

"Did he say anything to you as you left?"

"No. But he caught my arm and kissed me. And that was our last moment together."

Brianna covers her face with her hand. Judy reaches over and pats her shoulder. She composes herself.

"As I leave the room, I look down the hall toward the elevator. Its doors are open and Mrs. Pratt is standing there. Our eyes lock and neither of us move. Then I understood why Richard needed me to leave."

Ah yes. As old as Sarai and Hagar.

"I immediately turned the other direction. It was only a few steps to the stairs. I took them down to the parking garage and drove away."

We are quiet.

"I believe she killed him. I think she went to his room and they argued and she stabbed him, and in a panic she pushed him over the balcony so that it would look like he had fallen."

"But leave the murder weapon behind?"

"She was not a professional assassin, Mr. Mote. She was a desperate woman. She didn't calculate; she simply fled."

I look at Judy, hoping, for once, that she has something to say. How much of this has she taken in? One nice person—Brianna—has accused another nice person—Mrs. Pratt—of having murdered a third seemingly nice person. Does this create any tension in Judy's mind? Does it enter a compartment labeled "Nice People Who Do Not-Very-Nice Things"? I have such a compartment—and it has about six billion people in it, including me.

count us too were not very nice no not very nice at all

NINETEEN

I am getting jumpy again. The stomachaches are back. And the voices that wouldn't sing to Prufrock are singing to me. I need to flee.

Luckily I have an excuse.

Mrs. Pratt had talked about the first Mrs. Pratt in our meeting together. It now occurs to me that it might be useful to look up the first wife to see if there was anything from Pratt's past that could throw light on things. Mrs. Pratt didn't know much about his early life, other than what she told me about his first marriage, and that he'd grown up poor and was determined not to walk in those shoes again. Said he would quote Henry Ford to the effect that history is bunk, and made it clear he didn't appreciate unsolicited probing.

I call up Mrs. Pratt the Second, who provides a Memphis address for Mrs. Pratt the First. It came off the letter she had received from the first wife after Pratt's death.

I walk out of my bedroom one morning with the single conviction that nightfall will not find me in the state of Minnesota. There is no certainty of finding the first Mrs. Pratt, or of her talking to me if I do. In fact, it seems certain that she won't have the foggiest notion of who killed Pratt or who would ever want to.

No, there is more Jonah than Poirot in this impulse. It is a flight from my troubles more than a promising search for who deconstructed the deconstructionist. But it is something the Furies tell me I must do.

I don't know how Judy will respond to Operation Flee Nineveh. I try to sound my heartiest:

"Hey, Jude. What you say me and you take a trip?"

"Where to?"

"Oh, I don't know. Say, for instance … Memphis!"

"Memphis?"

"Yeah, Memphis." I widen my eyes like you do when you're trying to convince a little kid that the gift he just opened from grandma is just what he always wanted. It doesn't look good with Judy. I'm not sure if there is any file in her brain with the word Memphis on it. It looks to be a null set. Less meaningful than if I had said "muffins."

"You … you mean Mem … Memphis, the home of the … the King?"

"The King?"

"Why … Mr. El … Mr. Elvis Presley, silly."

Silly indeed. How can I have forgotten.

"That's right, Jude. The ol' hound dog himself."

"Mr. … Mr… . Mr. Swivel Hips?" Judy puts her hands on her own hips and gyrates them in circles, then breaks into self-congratulatory laughter.

"The very same. And we can visit his house while we're there." I start to say, "and see his grave," but I don't know whether Judy is aware of Elvis's passing. People sort of live in the eternal present for Judy, as she does herself. I don't want to slow the momentum of events by dragging in untimely departures.

"I would love to visit Mr. … Mr. Elvis Presley."

It is strange that Judy had grown up listening to Elvis, even his stuff from the '50s when he was a bat out of hell to people in our slice of America. That was a nice thing about our parents. They were quasi-fundamentalists, but only mildly infected, the fever tempered by wide reading and a love of music and general optimism about life. Not like Uncle Lester, who believed more in God's wrath than God did.

Before Judy and I were born, my parents had one of the first televisions that Satan sneaked into our neighborhood. (My dad loved Milton

Berle in drag.) They ran the not inconsiderable risk of being found in a movie theater when Jesus came back. And we even caught Mom and Dad dancing together in the living room late one night.

So even though Judy was just a tot when Elvis first wiggled his way through the Ed Sullivan Show (cameras instructed to stay above the waist), she discovered him soon enough, and a lifelong infatuation was born.

"He is a Christian man you know."

"I didn't know that."

"Oh yes. Sis … Sister Winifred told us. He sings songs about … about Jesus."

I have the Memphis address, two suitcases of clothes—his and hers—a huge bag of snack food, and a near-desperate need to be somewhere else. By noon we are on highway 52 out of St. Paul. The tank is full, our heads are empty, and the only requirement is to keep the nose of the car pointing south.

Judy is in high spirits and, at the moment, so am I.

"What do you think about this, Jude?"

"I … I think we are … we are on the road again."

"Just you and me."

"Like Pa … Pancho and Cisco."

"Like the Lone Ranger and Tonto."

"Like Bon … Bonnie and Clyde."

Bonnie and Clyde? She must have seen a rerun of that one after the nuns got booted.

Those nuns were a piece of work. The Sisters of the Good Shepherd first got their hands on Judy when she was fourteen or so. She was sent there not long after the insurance money came through. Turns out the drunk who killed our parents had deep pockets and it all went to us, which meant it went to whoever was taking care of us. The will, however, wasn't specific at all, and Lester figured out that if he sent Judy to an institution he would control her money for as long as she lived and my part until I was twenty-one.

So he was glad to see me join the army when I was seventeen, figuring, I suppose, that I might get myself killed in some lucky way. Turned out he blew all the money and had the good sense to die soon after, so Judy became a ward of the state and I became penniless, which completed the trifecta: penniless, clueless, and hopeless. A Trinity of Dysfunction.

So Judy went to Good Shepherd. The sisters were pre-Vatican II. In fact they were pre-Council of Trent. They figured if God had wanted the church to change, he would have informed them personally. The Latin Mass and head-to-toe habits were good enough for St. Julian of Norwich and they were good enough for them.

They also harkened back to a time before the takeover of caring by government and social scientists. When compassion moved from being a community virtue to a government program, the nuns were doomed, though it took them a while to get caught. These women simply did not understand the modern world. Like when the local inspector told Sister Brigit they were in violation of code because each resident did not have the required square footage of closet space. She reportedly answered, "Jesus said, 'Feed my sheep.' He didn't say anything about closet space."

The sisters did everything wrong, though most of it turned out right. They gave out whacks for misbehavior, not knowing that violence only breeds more violence. They gave everyone jobs to do without paying anyone a dime—workers of the world unite! They taught their charges to love and fear God, blind to the right of every American to believe in nothing. And they never developed a single program with the aim of raising the residents' self-esteem. It's no wonder the sisters were shut down. They were untrained, uncertified, unprogressive, uncompliant, and unrepentant. In sum, they were, well, too nun-ish.

Yes, the sisters certainly contributed to their own undoing. They didn't properly comprehend that they lived in a time in which Carl Sagan is taken to be a sage. (I mean if, as he claims, the cosmos is all we know and all we'll ever know, how the hell would he know that?) The best people are trying to rescue the disadvantaged from superstition, not subsidize it. These nuns weren't stupid, but they weren't savvy either. They once had the residents sing Christmas carols for the state compliance officer. Didn't they know that "Silent Night" can get you shut down faster than an outbreak of plague?

Finally, about five years ago, someone decided they had to get tough with these constitutional terrorists. The sisters were told that because they were a sectarian organization, they would no longer get the government per diem that goes with each resident. They either had to ditch the God talk or close it down. Eventually they turned things over to New Directions, a private, for-profit business that runs such institutions in twenty-six states. The nuns packed up their rosaries, kissed each of the residents goodbye, and headed for the cloister. The bureaucrats at the state Department of Human Services breathed a big sigh of relief. Finally, the residents were in the hands of professionals.

For better or worse, the professionals came in too late to have much effect on Judy. She had already been organized, systematized, and cate-chized. She knew when to sleep, when to eat, and when to pray. She knew where the silverware went, when the bus came, what to say to strangers, what time *Dragnet* reruns came on, and how to catch a gopher (her boy-friend, Ralph, taught her that). She knew how to separate the light from the dark in more ways than one. Which is to say she knew everything she needed to know. I wish I could say the same.

By the time we hit Rochester the travel high is subsiding. Judy senses it and begins to sing.

"Do Lord, oh do Lord, oh do remember me."

I'm not so far gone yet that I can't smile and join in.

"Do Lord, oh do Lord, oh do remember me."

I welcome the mindless repetition.

"Do Lord, oh do Lord, oh do remember me. Look away beyond the blue."

The next line takes me far beyond highway 52 heading for the Iowa border.

"I took Jesus as my Savior, you take him too. ... Look away beyond the blue."

Specifically, those words take me to a Wednesday night prayer meeting in a small church at a time when I was still wearing short pants and knee-high socks. Wouldn't you think people would get enough God-talk in four hours of church on Sunday, plus potluck? We had to go back for a midweek fix. It was a scene straight from Flannery O'Connor.

I see myself sitting in a pew on the right-hand side of our small church about halfway back. I'm studying the low-budget stained glass windows that fundamentalist churches used to have. No dramatic figures acting out Old Testament stories. That exceeded both the budget and our tolerance for iconography. Just panels of tepid colors clouding any view of the world outside. Why let oneself be distracted by reality?

The only attempt at art, beyond the Sallman Jesus hanging in the foyer, is the depiction of the Jordan River flowing into our sanctuary. The big, impossibly blue river, bounded by green trees and brown hills, snakes down the wall behind the choir loft and spills into our baptistry. You had to be impressed.

Never mind that the perspective of the painting was somehow simultaneously at ground level and from a helicopter at a thousand feet. I mean, it was a big challenge to get that river from the vertical wall to the horizontal baptistry without giving the congregation vertigo. Too much one way and the river looked like a waterfall, too much the other and all you saw was sky. I'd seen other Jordan Rivers, and I thought ours was up there with the best of them.

Anyhow, I'm looking back and forth between the Jordan and the stained glass when I hear the preacher saying, "Jesus died for you," with this big emphasis on "you." "Jesus died for *your* sins. Jesus died to set *you* free. Jesus died to give *you* eternal life."

I didn't like the idea at all. I never asked nobody to die for me. I never said I wanted to live forever. Set me free from what? The only part that made any sense was the stuff about sin. I was a little kid—at what passes for the age of innocence. What did I know of sin?

Plenty. I know this sounds sick, but I felt even as a little tyke that something was wrong with me. Something needed fixing and I wasn't going to be able to fix it myself. My God, it's embarrassing now to even hear myself rehearsing this. Sin. Salvation. Eternity. Throw in the terror of hellfire and you've got a strong case for child abuse. If I just knew who to sue.

At the time, though, I was only interested in making that broken feeling go away. And the preacher said the way to do that was to come forward to the front of the church while the people sang. And so the people sang and I went forward. I remember a little gasp coming from my mother's lips as I stepped out from the pew. She reached for me, but my dad put his hand on her forearm, and I was off down the aisle heading for eternity. And I remember feeling great, like this weight had been removed from my heart. I actually felt it in my chest, where the old pumper is. And I had no clear notion of what I was doing, except the preacher said to come forward and I was coming forward. And he shook my hand when I got to the front and he sat me down on the front pew and talked to me, and I can't remember what he said, but the next thing I know my mother and father are sitting there on either side and they're both crying, and I feel like I've done something really important and I'm glad about it. I am saved.

What I wouldn't give for that feeling today. Or even for the belief in the possibility of such a feeling. Saved. Grace. Forgiveness. Jesus. The vocabulary of faith—of one kind of faith. A language still spoken here and there. A hope still burning in some hearts. But not in mine. Not for many, many years. Not ever again.

We speed through Rochester without a glance—physicians, heal thyselves. Highway 52 turns into 63 and hence into Iowa. By now even Judy is out of songs. We have genuflected before the old rugged cross, marched in the Lord's army, experienced blessed assurance, and declared it is well with our souls. After all that, we are content for a while to let the farmhouses roll by.

Personally, I have always been happy to let things roll by. But I decide to use these miles of Iowa farmland to think. I will stake down what I know, list all the givens, factor in the variables, total up my columns, see what things add up to, and make a series of incisive, far-reaching decisions.

But first I need a snack.

"What's in the feed sack, Jude?"

"Well, let ... let us see."

Judy slowly pulls the grocery bag up from her feet on the car floor and even more slowly peers inside. She sticks her face almost entirely into the bag, wanting to answer this all-important question to the best of her ability. After a long pause, she responds, her voice muffled.

"Well, I ... I must say, Jon. I'm not sure wha ... what's in here. It ... it's dark."

"Try pulling things out."

"Yes, I think ... I think I will try pulling things out."

And so she does, and so we discover a delightful selection of the most useless food an unfettered market economy can produce. Worse than useless—deadly—but no less desirable for that. Besides, if usefulness were a requirement for existence, how many of us would still be around?

I choose the crunchy and salty over the sweet and sugary and then go back to my mental inventory. Let's see, what do I know about my life. I am on the wrong side of thirty-five, as our culture judges such things. I am separated from my wife, with divorce just a matter of me getting around to responding to the paperwork. I am living with my sister, who, despite substantial challenges, is far more acclimated to life than I am. I am of doubtful mental and emotional health. I am without a profession, and only sporadically employed. I have a soft belly before my time. I have no guiding philosophy of life or passionate beliefs. I get most of my opinions from cable television. I don't follow sports anymore, so I can't pretend to at least have a life when my team is winning. I belong to no clubs or organizations. (I quit the Y when I realized the fitness room was more competitive than the boardroom.) No pet has proved able to survive in my presence. I gave up my last hobby—collecting baseball cards—as a teenager when they quit packaging them with bubble gum. My parents are dead. I have no extended family members that I would want to be caught in the same photograph with except Judy.

And my stomach hurts. Often. And, oh yes, I hear voices. They do not wish me well.

Not an inspiring past, but it looks good compared to the future. I won't be able to fund a midlife crisis even if I've earned one. And after that, I'll have the same problems previously mentioned, only then I will also be old.

Right now, for instance, I haven't a single complaint about the state of my bowels. They function admirably, as God intended. How much longer will I be able to put that on my resume?

Then there are my employment prospects. I am currently accepting a woman's money in order to gather information that will be helpful in finding the person who murdered her husband. The only thing I have found, that her husband was having an affair, will just make her more miserable than she was before.

Perhaps I should ask for a raise.

We pass through Waterloo mid-afternoon. I successfully deflect any cheap symbolism for my own life. Then it is freeway to below Iowa City, where it turns into 218, another two-laner through America's stomach. I like being on the small roads. They feel more real than the freeways. Everyday, dirt-under-the-fingernails life is happening on either side— down this dirt driveway, in that field, outside yonder Dairy Queen.

Small roads are also a lot more honest about mortality. You glide down the interstate and most of the time you feel insulated from both life and death. But small roads are another matter. You feel the speed. Trees fly by twenty feet to your right, trucks four feet to your left. You pass the slow car on the curve because if you are right, as is likely, you will gain sixty seconds. If you are wrong, you will die, which has its silver linings. Almost every time you make it, because death is patient, knowing it gets plenty of chances.

Like the one it got with my mom and dad.

The farther south we travel, the farther we leave winter behind, at least the outer winter. Judy and I watch the snow give way to frozen

ground, then to panoramas of brown fields, then to mud and the occasional patch of green.

There's a shortcut off 218 that gets you to 61 without having to go
through Keokuk. Once on 61 I see the sign that says it's sixty miles to
Hannibal, Missouri. I smile—and know it is because of Huck Finn.

I didn't merely read about Huck Finn when I was a boy, I *was* Huck
Finn. At the least, I was his best friend. I was there with him and Tom
in the caves. I floated along with Huck and Jim down the Mississippi. I,
too, feared Indian Joe and squirmed under the civilizing efforts of Aunt
Polly. I was Huck Finn's best friend because I desperately needed a best
friend, and he was available.

In the years after my parents' death, I had to get away, and books were
the means to tunnel out. Out of my world, into another. Out of the fear
and turmoil, out of the sad darkness. Into a world where goodness often
won, where children sometimes laughed. Into the light.

And I not only lived in those stories, I learned *how* to live from them.
I learned that a Cyclops can be defeated by wiliness and a Philistine giant
overcome by courage and a sling, that the loss of liberty is more to be
feared than death, and that a yellow dog could teach us something about
self-sacrifice. I am unfit to be a professor of stories today. I had read too
much too soon with too much at stake to believe that stories are just
power moves.

It is late by the time we get to Hannibal. Before we look for a motel,
I decide to drive by the Mississippi. From the highway the streets fall
steeply down to the river. I park by a bluff along the water near a bridge.
Judy and I get out and walk along the bank. The river is wide at Hannibal, but not so wide that you can't clearly see the other side. It is a livable
vista, big enough to make you feel small, but not so big as to make you
feel insignificant.

There is a full moon low in the sky and its light splashes across the
waters, squandering beauty on a sleeping town. I try to see riverboats
paddling up the river, steam whistles screeching. I try to see women in

hoop skirts, bales of cotton, and running boys, me and Huck among them. I am not successful.

"Why … why are we stopping here, Jon?"

"Oh, just to stretch our legs and look at the river."

"Yes, this is like the Jor … the Jordan River. There's a picture of this in my … my very own Bible."

"I wish this was the Jordan, Jude. God knows I could use a Promised Land."

TWENTY

We spend the night in Hannibal, at a place called "Huck's Rest Motel" or something similarly depressing. It is flanked on one side by Indian Joe's Gifts and on the other by the Becky Thatcher Cafe. It makes me proud to be an English major and a capitalist.

Hannibal to Memphis is all interstate once you hit I-70 west of St. Louis. The second day of travel has none of the fizz of the first. The high spirits of escape give way to the dull reminder that there is none.

the mind is its own place we can do allusion too

No escape from what you're carrying along with you. The arch in St. Louis, seen in the distance, looks to me like the coil of a noose.

I-70 kisses I-55 and I-55 follows the Mississippi the rest of the way to Memphis. You never see the river after St. Louis, but the map tells you it's there, just to the east, beyond the fields. Sort of how sacred texts point to divinity—not visible, but just over there. Rumors of God. In this case that old brown god.

The closer we get to Memphis, the worse I feel. Anxious at Cape Girardeau, miserable by Marion. Why didn't I try calling the Memphis wife before leaving? Why did I just assume she would be there waiting for me? Why didn't it occur to me that she might not be willing to talk at all? Why am I so incapable of learning from experience?

It is early evening when we cross the bridge over the Mississippi into Memphis. The river looks muddy and slow and indifferent. I am trying to imagine that this is the same water that flowed past me in St. Paul. I try to take the lights hung all over the bridge as a hopeful sign, but it is going to take more than decorations to brighten me.

Pratt's first wife lives in a small town just east of Memphis called Collierville. It is in the process of becoming a suburb, but is unwilling to admit it. It has a classic town square with grass and flowers in the middle and the doomed hardware stores, meat markets, and the like on each side. The boutiques have already found this place, and the chain stores won't be far behind. An old barber shop sits off one corner of the square with a faded barber pole and an old Coca-Cola sign advertising refreshment for a dime.

I have the first Mrs. Pratt's address and her re-married name from her successor, so it isn't hard to find a phone number in the phone book. She is Mrs. Burket now, Barbara Burket. I am very nervous about calling her. I sit at the edge of the motel bed with my hand on the phone and look over at Judy as she studies the print of a crying clown's face that hangs above the television.

"This clown is … I should say, very sad, Jon."

I ignore the insight.

"Do you think she'll talk to us, Jude?"

"Why … why of course … of course she will talk to us, you silly boy. She … she is a very nice lady."

Judy attributes niceness to everyone until proven otherwise. It is her default setting for personal evaluations. Maybe something to be said for it.

And she is right. There is a long silence on the phone after I explain to Mrs. Burket who I am and what I am here for. Then she speaks quietly and slowly, obviously with a mind suddenly full of the past.

"I was real upset when I heard Dickie had been killed. It was a shock, you know? I still think about him ever so often and I just get sad. Dickie was my first love. I hated him for a while, but I got over that. It was really hard when I heard that he had died."

"Yes ma'am." I can't help sounding like Sergeant Friday.

"I don't think there's anything I could tell you that would help find who killed him."

"We're just looking for some background, Mrs. Burket. You never know what's going to turn out to be helpful."

"Well, in that case, I'd be willing to talk with you if you think it might do some good."

"It might do some good."

Only as I approach her door the next morning does it occur to me that I haven't done anything to prepare for this. I haven't made a list of questions. I don't know what I want to find out. Worse yet, I look at my reflection in the glass storm door and realize I am wearing dirty jeans and a plaid lumberjack shirt. I am an embarrassment to myself, to my sister, to God, to ex-husbands, and to popcorn researchers.

There is only one thing to do. Retreat. I take Judy by the hand and turn to go while the going is good. Just then the front door opens and Barbara Burket appears in a nicely pressed cotton dress. She is slim and attractive, her blond hair done in a little flip that dates her as early Mary Tyler Moore.

"Mr. Mote?"

I am about to say "No" when Judy chimes in.

"Hello. My ... my name is Judith Mote. And ... and this here is my very own bro ... brother of mine, Jon. We are here to see you."

Tonto my eye. More like Delilah.

I think if I'd come by myself, Mrs. Burket wouldn't have let me in. But she smiles at Judy and steps aside as she holds open the door.

"Well if you're here to see me, then this is the way in."

Her home is everything that Pratt's isn't. She has brown shag carpet, an olive green sofa and chairs—two different shades of orange—and cardboard prints of vaguely inspirational mountain scenes. A plaque of copper praying hands hangs near the entryway with the words "Prayer Changes Things" embossed across it.

She motions for Judy and me to sit on the sofa. I am feeling more scattered than the Jews of the Diaspora. Each thought is independent of those on either side, and none of them have anything to do with the situation at hand.

Judy sees that I am paralyzed and does her best to rescue me.

"Did you … did you ever know … Mr. Elvis Presley?"

Mrs. Burket smiles.

"No, I never did meet Mr. Presley. He died not long after I came to Memphis."

"Yes, he had a very … I should say, a very tragic life."

Where Judy got the phrase "a very tragic life" I have no idea. But I know I need to jump in here before she moves to a follow-up question about the Bee Gees.

"Please excuse me, Mrs. Burket, for being so awkward here. Like I said on the phone last night, I'm not a detective or investigator or anything like that. Mrs. Pratt … that is Dr. Pratt's wife, his second wife that is … well, anyway, she just hired me to … well … to look into things, so … well …"

I am in no shape to be talking to strangers. I am barely able to follow inhale with exhale. Starting and finishing sentences is a bridge too far. I am on the edge of standing and walking out with a simple "I'm sorry" and it must show on my face.

"Mr. Mote. Why don't you take it easy for a moment? You're just off to a bad start. I know a thing or two about bad starts. You've come a long way, so why don't we try to make it worth something. I'll just talk about Dickie and me for a bit and you see if any of it seems helpful. How bout that?"

Mercy drops round us are falling. I nod and she starts off. Only God knows where she's going to end up.

"Dickie and I knew each other all our lives. We only lived three blocks apart growing up. His brothers used to fight with my brothers. For a while we went to the same church together, but then the church split and his family went with the breakaway group and we stayed. We started going out when I was fourteen. Dickie was fifteen. I thought he was really old. Can you imagine that, thinking fifteen was old?

"Dickie was so cute and so nice. He was the only boy I ever went out with, the only one. His hair was black and curly. I used to wrap it around my finger to make little ringlets on his forehead. He pretended to hate it, but he liked me sitting in his lap and fussing over him. Seems he always needed a woman fussing over him."

I look at her closely to see if this is a storm warning, but she seems lost in pleasant memories.

"We dated all through high school. Nobody thought of one of us without thinking of the other. We were perfect for each other. Everybody said so. Everybody knew we would get married someday.

"Dickie was a wonderful athlete, you know. He was good at anything he tried. He used to say he wanted to be a coach someday. Said he thought it would be great to have a job where he could work with kids and be outside. A lot of people were surprised, in fact, when he decided to go to college. You know, not so many kids went to college back then. We lived in a small town near the river in Louisiana. St. Francis can't have been more than fifteen-hundred when we were growing up, even smaller now. You really only had a few kids going to college, and everybody knew who they would be by ninth grade. I don't think anyone thought Dickie would be one of them, certainly no one in his family.

"Those Pratts weren't known for sending kids to college. Reform school maybe. No, I'm just kidding. Maybe one or two of Dickie's cousins got in trouble, but the Pratts were basically just trying to make it like everybody else."

I feel composed enough now to make a contribution.

"I understand Dr. Pratt grew up in poverty."

She laughs.

"Did Dickie say that?"

"He seemed to suggest it from time to time."

"Dickie's family wasn't any more or less poor than the rest of us, which is to say they didn't have any extra money, but they weren't missing any meals either. Looking back now, it's not too hard to maybe convince yourself you were poor, if you make a list of all the things you didn't have.

But half those things hadn't been invented at the time and the other half no one else had either, so it didn't matter much."

"What was he like then—in high school?" I know I am asking this for myself, not for anything useful.

"Like I say, Dickie was the nicest guy. He was real sweet. He was just a regular kid. He treated me great. He never put me down in front of his friends like a lot of guys did with their girlfriends. My parents loved him. He was so polite. He called them Mr. and Mrs. Ford even after we were married."

"How did he do in school?"

"He was smart, but he never let on much. He did enough to keep the teachers happy, but not so much as to get a reputation, if you know what I mean. I don't think even he knew then how smart he really was. I'm not sure it did him a lot of good when he found out."

"When did you two get married?"

"The weekend after our high school graduation. Dickie's best man was going into the army right away and we wanted him in the wedding. There didn't seem any reason to wait. We were done with high school, and Dickie had lined up a real good summer job working for the county. And I'd been doing sales at the Clothes Barn all through high school and they were going to make me an assistant manager. Looks like small potatoes now, of course, but it seemed good to us then."

She stops a moment and starts twisting the hair at her right temple around her finger, looking off out the window at another time and place.

"A lot of things looked good to us then that didn't look so good to Dickie later. I guess I was one of them."

This is not a white place on the map I want to explore. I'm not up to probing decades-old wounds from a long-dead marriage. I know well enough that nothing painful is ever dead, only dormant, waiting with geological patience for a tiny fissure to start the lava flowing.

"How is it Dr. Pratt ended up going to college?"

"Basketball. There was a coach who heard about Dickie and he called one day not long after we were married and asked if Dickie wanted to play ball for him. Said he could make it work cost-wise and it would be a great opportunity. So Dickie asked me what I thought, and I said why not, and so we went off to college. Or at least Dickie did. I went along to work and keep house."

I'm happy the ball is rolling this way and decide to give it another push.

"When Dr. Pratt was in college, or later in graduate school or in those first few years of teaching, did he make any serious enemies? I mean, did he ever have any falling-outs with people over money or inheritances, or maybe even drugs, or anything that you can remember?"

I want to add "wives or girlfriends" to the list, but I figure she will include that on her own.

"You know, I really think Dickie's enemy-making days didn't start until he did his makeover."

"Makeover?"

"That's what I called it. You know how in these women's magazines they show how somebody looked before and then they change their hair and their makeup and their clothes and they just look like a totally different person? Well that's what happened to Dickie. He had a makeover. It's like he just decided he wasn't going to be Dickie Pratt from St. Francis anymore. He got rid of his accent, his clothes, his car …"

She hesitates for a few moments, then finishes the sentence to herself.

"… and then he got rid of me."

I want to offer words of consolation or deflection, but none come to mind.

"You know, Dickie had this great sense of humor when we were growing up. He made me laugh all the time. But in graduate school he stopped being funny and started being, I don't know … witty. And, you know, Mr. Mote, that's not the same thing. He had some clever remark about everything I said, and somehow it usually left me feeling stupid. I couldn't make a passing comment on the weather without him analyzing it and finding it ridiculous.

"And then one day he came home and said from now on I had to call him Richard. Imagine that. I mean he had been introducing himself as Richard for quite a while, but I was his wife. I had known him since he wore his hair in a flattop. He'd been Dickie to me forever. Why did *I* have to change? Why couldn't I call him Dickie at home and the rest of the world call him whatever he wanted?

"And then he goes into this big thing about language and words making reality or something, and he got really mad about it. And so of course I started calling him Richard. I think maybe that was the beginning of the end. I still loved him, but he wasn't Dickie Pratt anymore and he didn't want to be."

I can identify.

"What do you mean when you say it was after the … well, the makeover, that he started making enemies?"

"Oh, I don't know. I don't mean real enemies. It was kind of strange. I grew up in church in a small town, so I know all about petty rivalries and talking behind people's backs, all the time singing harmony on the hymns and being active on the prayer chain. But I never quite saw anything to match how those university people broke into their little cliques and then cut each other up every which way."

Mrs. Pratt was right. This woman is not stupid.

"At first Dickie tried to stay clear of all that stuff. But he found no one was allowed to be neutral. You either joined one camp or another or they all attacked you—or ignored you, which for Dickie was even worse. So he went to battle for whichever group he was in, and once he tasted a little blood, he found out that he liked the taste. And he was as good at that sport as he was at the others. I think the same bandy rooster feistiness that made him a good point guard in basketball also made him good at all that academic infighting."

Her reference to Pratt's shortness calls to mind my long-held theory about short men and mass murder, but now is not the time.

"So you're saying he made the usual ideological enemies during those years, but no one you know of who would really wish him harm?"

"Not physical harm. That's right."

I don't know what else to ask. I can undoubtedly find out more about the Richard née Dickie Pratt of St. Francis, but Barbara Burket apparently knows nothing that will be helpful in finding out who killed him.

The Dickie Pratt she knew died long before that night in the hotel room in Minneapolis.

I look over at Judy, who has been content during this time to think her own thoughts. I am sorry to have wasted Mrs. Pratt's money. I also don't look forward to the long drive home. I'm not feeling well and have no prospects of feeling better.

"Is there anything else you can think of that might be helpful? Any little thing or person that may have seemed unimportant at the time?"

"I don't think so."

"Well, I appreciate your willingness to talk to us, Mrs. Burket. And I apologize again for not giving you much advance warning."

I stand as I am saying this and so does Mrs. Burket. Judy catches the cue, slides off her chair, and runs the tape marked "Parting Pleasantries."

"I ... I too would ... would like to thank you for ... for a very nice time. We must do this again ... sometime."

Judy holds out her hand to Mrs. Burket, who shakes it with conviction and responds in kind.

"I would like that very much, Judith. It has been a pleasure having you in my home."

Then Mrs. Burket turns to me, and I am startled by a look of desperate suffering on her face. She knots her hands together at her waist and looks at her feet as she speaks.

"There is ... there may be one man who wanted Dickie dead. A whole family really. I doubt very much that any of them killed him, but they certainly had a reason."

I motion for Judy to sit down again. This seems to confuse her. Rising, thank yous, and handshakes are always followed by departures, not by sitting down again. It's like a clock going from twelve to one and then back to twelve. I am a little shaken myself. Mrs. Burket is starting to cry quietly.

"I've never told anyone this. My husband, Tremper, doesn't even know. It happened more than thirty-five years ago, but it haunts me more today than ever. I think about it every week. I dream about it two or three times a month. I've asked God to forgive me a thousand times and I guess he does, but I can't forgive myself."

I can tell I won't need to ask any prompting questions.

"I was only sixteen. My God, sixteen. That seems impossibly young. Was I ever sixteen?"

I look at Judy and can tell she is about to make a pronouncement about being sixteen. I catch her eye and shake my head. She snaps her mouth shut and slowly puts her finger to her lips. Message received.

"It was one of those hot, muggy summer nights in St. Francis where you just want to sit in front of a fan and not move a muscle. Dickie and I were downtown to the movie. I was wearing my white cotton dress with the spaghetti straps. It was my favorite dress when it was hot, and Dickie liked me in it."

I know she is stalling. You don't dream three times a month about white cotton dresses.

"We were walking home and Dickie and I start arguing. I accused him of giving the eye to another girl at the movie theater. And being sixteen I had a great flair for the dramatic, you know. He says he wasn't giving anybody any eye, but adds she *was* good-looking. So I say if he's so interested in how other girls look, I'm going to walk home by myself, thank you very much. So I run ahead about twenty yards and then start walking again. Far enough to be away from him but close enough so he can still see me even in the dark.

"And of course what I want him to do is run and catch up to me and say again that he wasn't looking at any girl and for me to be reasonable. But just as I'm sixteen and dramatic, he's seventeen and prideful. So he just hangs back and says nothing. And we're out of the downtown lights by now and it's very dark. And I'm walking by the lumberyard fence where you turn right at the corner to go to my house. And I'm hurrying because I want to get around the corner and out of sight of Dickie so that maybe he worries about me a little. And ... oh my God. I don't know if I can go on."

She puts her head in her hands and starts crying hard. Judy gets up and walks over to her and pats her on the back. Judy looks at me and puts a finger to her lips to show she knows not to say anything. Mrs. Burket pulls a tissue out of her dress pocket and wipes her face. After a few moments, she starts to talk again.

"So I'm rushing around the corner in the dark and I run into this huge man. Really run into him. And he kind of embraces me, or pushes me away, or protects himself against me running into him, I don't know what. I fall down. I have never been so shocked and terrified in my entire life and I freeze for a moment and then I begin to scream and scream and scream and scream."

She looks like she wants to scream right now.

"And I remember him saying, 'No miss, don't do that. I'm sorry miss. It was an accident. Please don't holler.' But I just kept on screaming, and then he was gone. Dickie of course was running toward the screams, and this man comes running around the corner past him, and I can hear Dickie's voice now, 'You, nigger, stop!' But he didn't stop and I don't blame him. Dickie came on around the corner and found me sitting there on the ground.

"By now porch lights were going on all down the street. A man came running out of the nearest house carrying a rifle. Dickie was down on his knees holding me and asking was I okay. I had stopped screaming but couldn't talk because I was sobbing so hard I could hardly get my breath.

"Two or three other men arrived about the same time as the guy carrying the rifle. Their wives and kids were standing on the porches and behind the screen doors. The men asked what happened. I was starting to calm myself down. I wanted to say I had run into this strange man and I was okay, but I couldn't talk. Then Dickie said, 'A nigger jumped my girlfriend and was trying to molest her.' One of the men said, 'A nigger? You sure it was a nigger?' Then Dickie said, 'I'm sure. And I know which nigger it was.'

"So they led me up to one of the houses, and the women met me on the lawn and put their arms around me and started yelling orders out to their kids behind the screen doors. And when I got into the light of the porch one of the women gasped and pointed at my dress. I looked down and there was a greasy handprint on my left breast. And a couple of the women turned and looked at Dickie with looks that would kill. The man with the rifle saw them looking and said, 'It wasn't him. It was a nigger.' Then all the women stiffened up and swept me into the house."

Mrs. Burket stands up and paces around the room. She hugs her waist with her arms, one forearm above the other, a defensive stance I first noticed in girls when I was a boy.

"While the women fussed over me, the men talked with Dickie on the porch. They took us home that night in a car and talked with my parents, who thanked them for their neighborliness. I thought it was all over, but Dickie came over the next day and I never saw him so upset. He told me the huge man I had run into was really Johnnie Roberts. I didn't believe it. Johnnie Roberts was only eighteen and not much bigger than Dickie. His daddy ran a general store in the colored section. I told Dickie the man I ran into was twice as big as Johnnie Roberts, but Dickie said that any black man looks twice as big in the dark to a white girl on her own. So I said, so what if it was Johnnie Roberts. It was over now and I didn't want to talk about it.

"But Dickie said, 'You think it's over, Barbara, but it's just startin'.' And I said what do you mean it's just starting, and he says that a couple of those men from last night are real upset and they're talking to some other men in town and from other places and they're saying the niggers in St. Francis need to be taught a lesson and that the lesson was going to start with Johnnie Roberts.

"And I told Dickie that he was going to have to stop them. I told him, like I had when I whispered to him in the car the night before, that it was an accident, that we just ran into each other in the dark, and that nobody should be hurt because of it. But Dickie said it was too late for that, that he'd already said what he said last night and that he couldn't take it back. These were men, and some pretty rough men at that, and he was a seventeen-year-old kid and what could he do? And I said he could tell the truth, tell them what really happened, and he said, they don't want to know what really happened. All they know is that the niggers need to be taught a lesson and this is as good an opportunity as any. It wouldn't do any good to change the story now.

"And I cried and begged him, but he refused, and so I said I was going to tell them myself. And he said 'If you do that, Barbara, I will never talk to you again and I will tell everybody you are a slut, and they will believe it. I'm not going to have you make me look bad.' Why I didn't see right then …"

She pauses but never finishes the sentence.

"But I shut my mouth and didn't say a word, and so I'm just as guilty for what happened as the guy who held the rope."

I have known where Mrs. Burket's story was heading for the last few minutes and I don't really want to hear the end. I don't want to put her through the telling, which is obviously devastating to her, and I don't like the feeling that is rising in me. I have felt it before. But as I start to tell her she needn't go on, she gets up and goes down the hall, saying she will be back in a second.

I look at Judy.

"He … he is not a nice person."

Bingo.

After what seems a long time, Mrs. Burket comes back with a letter box. She sits down and puts it carefully on her lap, like a holy relic.

"My husband does not know about this box. No one does. I haven't opened it in years, but I know everything in here by heart. It's stuff from when Dickie and me were together, mostly from high school. His varsity letter is in here. And the dried corsage he gave me for prom. And letters we wrote to each other when I was away for part of the summer after my sophomore year. And our wedding invitation."

She opens the box and looks at the contents stacked there, then digs down to the bottom and pulls out a black-and-white photograph and a yellowed newspaper clipping. She starts talking again, but like a young child repeating lines memorized for a school program—flat and expressionless, seemingly without emotion, because the only felt emotion is bottomless regret.

"It was two nights after I ran into Johnnie Roberts. They found Dickie walking home from my house around ten o'clock. They were in three cars and a pickup. They told him to come along. He said he couldn't, that he had to get home, but they said it was his girl that got molested and it was his duty to be part of making things right. I think they thought having him along gave them a kind of protection if the law got wind of it.

"They went to Johnnie Roberts' house and his daddy said Johnnie wasn't there and that he hadn't done nothing wrong. But they said they would decide what was right and wrong, and they found Johnnie hiding in a toolshed in the back. And they drug him to the pickup and threw him in the back, and four or five guys jumped on top of him to keep him down. And Johnnie's mother was screaming his name in the yard, Dickie said, but some of the men had shotguns and they held the family back.

"Dickie would never tell me what exactly happened in the woods, and that was okay because I didn't want to know. But when we got divorced … well, you know, I was really hurt and angry. And I had this lawyer who was a friend of my family and was going to be sure Dickie was going to live up to the alimony agreement, which at first Dickie said was just words on a piece of paper and had no significance for him. So my lawyer calls me in one day and lays this photograph in front of me and says, 'I don't think we have to worry about those alimony payments anymore.'"

She reaches over and hands me the photograph. It is a posed group picture. Forty or fifty men and boys stand in ragged rows facing the camera, the ones in back standing on a rise. Many of them are smiling, others have the stern look of Civil War portraits. On the right-hand side, almost neglected, an afterthought, is the hanging body of a young black man, his head cocked to the side under the rope that disappears out of the top of the photograph. He is shirtless, and his pants are opened at the zipper, dark stains running down the legs.

I want to throw up.

"That's Dickie just below Johnnie Roberts' feet."

Sure enough. Standing just below the body, between two grinning men, is the young Richard Pratt. He isn't smiling. He isn't frowning. He is blank, perhaps in shock, perhaps just empty, ready to be filled.

"And here's the clipping from the local paper that came out the next afternoon."

I reach over and take it from her hand. It is in a style of type you don't see in papers anymore. The small headline reads, "Local Negro Commits Suicide in Woods." Jouissance indeed.

TWENTY-ONE

The drive back from Memphis to Minnesota feels much longer—in time and in implication—than the drive down. No singing, no snacks, only flat roads and dark thoughts.

My thoughts are about the morphing of Dickie Pratt—athlete, good kid, popular, shallow—into Dr. Richard Pratt—intellectual, activist, celebrated, sophisticated. Yes, sophisticated, as in Sophist-like, and very deep. It doesn't require much genius to see why he would be hungry for a view of reality that let him remake himself—remake the world. Behold, old things are passed away; all things are become new. He had converted to a new religion, one that promised him a new kind of absolution from his sins, not least by dismissing the idea that there were sins to be absolved from. No fixed boundaries, no metanarratives, no sin, and, voila, no guilt.

It's a game I am trying to play myself. But I've never been very good at games. A line from Melville comes to mind that I cited in my failed dissertation: "Lamps are extinguished by those annoyed by the light"—or something like that.

Not all my thoughts are so abstract. I am also trying to decide how much to tell Mrs. Pratt. One part of me wants to tell her everything—to justify the money she is spending on me and on this trip, and to show her that in the long orbit of my life I sometimes swing close to the sun of competence. She has hired me to "look into things" and I have looked.

Into the abyss, you might say. I am trying to pull myself back from the edge, but the darkness is calling my name.

As usual, the part of me that wants to do something is opposed by the part that wants to wait. Dickie Pratt is dead, killed by Richard Pratt. Now Richard Pratt is dead, killed by who knows who. Why kill Richard Pratt a second time, even more cruelly, in the mind and heart of his widow? She thinks him a good man; what is accomplished by her thinking otherwise? How is anyone better for it? And who is left to say he wasn't a good man—all things considered—except maybe someone like Judy, whose standards are not common in the modern world?

I never knew Dickie Pratt. The Richard Pratt I knew had been good to me, even when he was counseling me to abandon my future. I feel a kind of kinship with him, a kind of loyalty. He had something in his past of which he was profoundly ashamed—at a level which no ideology could soothe. I know something about shame.

Anyway, I decide that for the time being I'm not going to say anything about Johnnie Roberts and that photograph to Mrs. Pratt. I'll do a good deed by not doing anything. If there are sins of omission, maybe there are mercies of omission too. I declare myself Saint Inert the Avoider.

Because we don't leave Memphis until the afternoon, we only make it to Festus, Missouri, before I can't drive any farther. We find a motel that was built back when people knew where the word "motel" came from. All the rooms are on ground level, opening onto the parking lot. I pull the car up in front of door eight, giving the people inside a nice taste of our headlights.

Our room is smoky and damp, a pleasant combination. I am thankful for the dim lights. What you don't see won't nauseate you.

Or maybe it will. Because my stomach is starting to hurt again, and I know it's not just the junk food we've been eating. I lie in the motel bed trying not to think of Dickie Pratt or Johnnie Roberts or that photograph. I try to think about the moon on the Mississippi as a prelude to not thinking at all, when a phantom appears in the darkness. It's Huck's pappy, only worse.

This phantom floats up toward the surface like the ugly head of a giant catfish rising from the darkness of a deep pool. I try pushing it back down, but it is insistent, predatory. With its rising comes a feeling of dread and revulsion. I break into a dank sweat.

I can see the door to Judy's bedroom at the top of the stairs in the small house we grew up in. I again see myself as a kid climbing up the stairs. I want to yell to myself to turn around, not to open the door, not to see, not to be seen. I try to break the tape that is running in my head, to send the catfish back into the darkness before its spiky head breaks the surface. But this time it will not go back. This time the boy gets to the top of the stairs

we told you not to go up those stairs

and hears the muffled grunts coming from behind the bedroom door

but you dont pay no attention to us

and he walks over to it and reaches for the doorknob as he has innocently done so many times before and pushes it open

well then go ahead

and walks over the threshold from one life into another.

see how you like it

There is Judy lying on the bed, though all I can actually see of her are the white ruffles of the pile of petticoats pushed up over her head. Kneeling in the middle of her petticoats and between her legs is Uncle Lester, thrusting himself into the pile of white and making horrible little grunts, his head cocked back and his eyes closed. I want to back out of the door or drop through the floor or simply melt into the air, but I am as rooted as the Himalayas. Judy's face rises from the other side of the petticoats, a mask of uncomprehending terror. She whispers my name— "Jon"—an identification and an appeal, then disappears again behind the petticoats. Uncle Lester instantly steps off her and swings a long arm toward me, catching me by the shirt front. He looks like a demon, his face a knot of lust and anger and fear. He pulls me close with one hand while he works on his zipper with the other. "You didn't see nothing, boy. You hear me? You didn't see nothing." He tries talking into my face, but I keep my chin down and look directly into his neck. I want to close my eyes but they won't even blink. All I can see is his pointy Adam's apple moving up and down, up and down, like a bobber on a fishing line floating on the ripples of the river. "You say a word about this, boy, even one little squeak, and I will kill you. And then I will kill Judy. And then I will kill myself. You understand? I will kill us all. I will kill us all. I will kill us all." Up and down, up and down, like a bobber.

I lie in the motel bed the rest of the night, frozen. The nausea is still strong in the morning. My paper-thin sanity depends on getting out of that room as quickly as possible, but I have a strong aversion to going back to St. Paul and the houseboat on the river. I know that wherever I go, that catfish head is coming along.

I wonder what Pratt would say about that catfish. Was it remembered or manufactured? Transubstantiation or consubstantiation or mere symbol? Would he say it referred to something that really happened? Or is putting *really* before *happened* some kind of nostalgic holdover from a more naive age? Was it nothing more than an electro-molecular event in a lobe of my brain? Can we say anything absolute about it—or do we only have attitudes toward it, cultural configurations? Am I allowed to think my uncle Lester was an evil bastard who should burn in hell? On what basis?

I get into the car with no plan and no ability to plan. Judy knows something is up but hasn't yet decided how to respond. She rubs her hands anxiously and looks at the sky out the passenger window. When I get to the edge of the parking lot, the car turns north again, and I accept it.

Judy is mostly quiet throughout the long day of driving, but it's clear she has read the handwriting on the wall and believes it is time to distance herself from Belshazzar.

mene mene

As we approach the southern limits of St. Paul late in the day, she announces that she has come to a decision.

"I think … I should say, I think, Jon, that I should go back."

"We're almost home, Judy. Just a few more minutes."

"No, Jon. I think I should go back … back to my friends."

I feel sick, hearing from her mouth what I have already set in motion. I should be happy that she wants to do what I have been dreading having to tell her she must do, but I feel abandoned instead.

"Why back there, Jude? Aren't we having a good time together? Isn't this better than … well, isn't it better?"

"I like … I like being with you very much, Jon. You … you are my brother of mine. But you … you are not always your own self."

"What does that mean, Jude?"

you know what it means you have always known what it means we are getting bigger every day bigger every day

"Sometimes you are your own self and some … sometimes you are not your own self. And your not your own self … well, I should say, your not your own self is not … is not a very nice person."

Who can argue with that?

She's right of course. It's the best thing for her. I'm sliding toward the dark and the pace is picking up. I need to get her back to a safe place.

I know, of course, that when she goes, I go.

TWENTY-TWO

By the time we get back to St. Paul, Mrs. Pratt has left town for a while, so I have an opportunity to fall apart without fear of disturbance. And I seize it. I've always had only one plodding gear for moving forward, but multiple reverse gears—fast, faster, and abandon ship. I'm currently in second-gear reverse, heading toward third.

Still, there are days I can function, and so I do. Like I've said, I should get much more credit for getting out of bed and walking out the door than I'm given. And on one of those high-performance days I return to the scene of the crime.

"I just want someone besides me to know the truth." Brianna's words have been bouncing around in my head since our talk. A strange thing for a self-proclaimed kindred spirit of Pratt's to say. If he were still around, I'm sure he'd correct it—gently and lovingly of course.

What to make of her conviction that Mrs. Pratt was the killer? It might be rationally plausible, but it doesn't feel emotionally plausible. Sort of what the idea of God became for me as I got older.

But had Mrs. Pratt in fact been at the hotel that night? Maybe Brianna Jones does "know the truth," but I don't. I am going to have to keep looking. I am going to have to pay a visit to my friend at the Minneapolis Marriot.

Okay, so it's a stretch to call Mark a friend. We were, once upon a time, fellow witnesses to our mutual failures. He'd been in the grad program at the university the same time I was. He never finished either, but had a better excuse. His wife got pregnant with twins and he had to drop out. He was already working at the hotel, so he just went full-time. You might think he would be disappointed to be hailing cabs rather than lecturing on postcolonial hegemony, but he claimed to be quite content.

"There are worse jobs than opening doors for people, Jon. I could be a tobacco company exec or making landmines. Nobody is worse off in the world because of what I do. Millions of people can't say the same, including a few in the English department."

Makes sense. An opened door, a smile, a helpful direction or two. A clear contribution to the common good, even if a tip was expected. What don't you pay for in this life?

I tell him when I call that I've been hired to look into Pratt's murder. He laughs. Says there's poetic justice in me looking for the killer of the guy who killed my academic career. I say I never thought of Pratt as having killed my career. I'm pretty sure I murdered it myself. He just laughs again.

We meet across the street from the hotel to talk over coffee and scones before he starts his shift.

"Yeah, I worked that night. Held the door for some of my old profs, but none of them recognized me—or at least didn't admit to it. Not even Ms. Smith-Corona. I bet I'm the only student who ever handed her a paper with the title, 'Gynecological Images in *Alice in Wonderland*.' You'd think she'd remember me for that."

I tear my napkin into little strips while Mark talks. I don't know how long to pretend to be interested in the details of his life before I get to the two or three questions I want to ask. When he starts on how lousy he's felt since his operation, I jump in.

"Did you see anything the night Pratt was murdered that might shed some light on who killed him?"

"Well, I saw you."

"I'm not surprised you saw *me*. I was there to hear Pratt's talk. I mean, did you see anybody looking … oh I don't know … looking … "

"… like someone who wanted to kill a literary theorist? What exactly is that look?"

"Okay, okay. Let me ask you another question. Did you by any chance see Pratt's wife that night?"

"Sure."

"Wait. You did? Mrs. Pratt? That same night?"

"Sure. I saw her come in and I saw her go out."

"What times?"

"I don't know. She wasn't there long. It was late, a long time after the banquet. Maybe eleven o'clock or so."

"Are you absolutely sure it was her? Do you know what she looks like?"

"Listen, Jon. You ask me if I'd seen her and I say 'yes,' then you ask me if I know what she looks like. I know what she looks like. I saw her plenty of times when we were at the U, including a couple of times at their house when Pratt had classes over. Do you want me to describe her to you? What's the big deal?"

"Okay. I'm sorry. You saw her. That's good, I guess. Now, did you notice anything particular about how she looked? Her mood, the expression on her face—anything like that?"

"Yeah, I noticed. I make it a point to look customers in the eye. It helps with the tips. She had this, I guess you could say, sort of suppressed smile when she arrived, like she was anticipating something."

"And when she came out?"

"She looked like Medusa on a bad hair day. Really pale. You could tell she was trying not to cry."

"Didn't that seem strange to you?"

"Why strange? A lot of people go through life trying not to cry. It wasn't any business of mine."

"What did she do when she left?"

"Jumped in the first taxi in line and was gone. Might have even been the same taxi that dropped her off. She couldn't have been in the hotel more than ten minutes. In and out … like our academic careers, eh Jon?"

"Yes, in and out. Very good. Was she carrying anything with her?"

"Hmm, I don't know. Not any big luggage, because I remember there was nothing for me to help her with. Maybe a small overnight bag. I'm not sure."

I sit there for a few moments, stunned. Brianna was right. Mrs. Pratt had been to the hotel that night. Why hadn't she told me? She hadn't denied being there, but she hadn't brought it up either. It's suspicious as hell.

"But you know, Jon. Mrs. Pratt isn't the only one with some explaining to do."

"What do you mean?"

"You should talk to Maria."

"Who's Maria?"

Mark leans forward in his chair and nods, as if to say, "Wouldn't you like to know?" He is obviously feeling conspiratorial, enjoying the role of star informer.

"She's in housekeeping at the hotel. She's working right now. I haven't talked to her about it myself, but I hear she found something very interesting in the luggage of one of the guests on the night Pratt was murdered."

"Something very interesting?"

"Something very interesting."

"On the night Pratt was murdered?"

"On the night he was murdered."

"What was it?"

"Ask Maria."

So I ask Maria. Mark takes me across the street and we find her in the linen room. She is small, dark, and in her twenties. She speaks English like I speak German—hunting for words like a lost ten-dollar bill.

Mark does the talking at first in tourist Spanish. When he tells her I am looking into Pratt's murder, she turns whiter than the sheets she's holding.

"No policía, no policía. I know nada about nada, please."

"Tell her I'm not from the police."

"I told her that. I think. Or maybe I told her you weren't a parakeet. I don't know."

I regret having spent my time in high school Spanish staring longingly at Tina Steiner. I decide I can miscommunicate as well as Mark.

"Yo estoy un amigo de la esposa … del … del hombre muerto." Ser or estar? "No estoy de la policía. Yo necesito su ayuda."

She stares at me.

"Por favor."

She takes pity on me and on my Spanish.

"Okay. You want about the gun, no?"

I don't know what she's talking about but I want to sound encouraging.

"Yes, please tell me about the gun."

"I turning back bed in man's room. Suitcase is open. I no touch nada in suitcase. I honest. I need job. I nunca take nothing."

"Yes, I understand."

"But I see something in suitcase."

"What did you see?"

"Pistola."

"A gun?"

"Sí, a gun."

"Did you touch it or tell anyone?"

"No. I no touch the gun. It not for me to worry. I see guns before. Pero más tarde, when I hear about kill that night, I think maybe gun."

"So you saw this gun in Pratt's room on the night he was killed?"

"No. No la habitación del muerto. Otra habitación."

"Another room? Not Pratt's?"

"Sí. I write número and later ask Enrique at desk."

"What was the name of the person who had the gun?"

She sets down her linens and walks over to a battered desk by the door. She takes a pencil and a pad of paper and prints out a name and hands it to me.

"This his nombre."

I look at the name in neat block letters.

"Daniel Abramson?"

"Sí, like in la Biblia."

Life, as usual, is giving me more than I budgeted for. I now not only have confirmation that Mrs. Pratt was at the hotel that night long enough to kill her husband (and was very distraught when she left), but that Abramson, Mrs. Pratt's number one suspect, was also there, and that he had a gun. Abramson is the last person in the world to carry a gun. It would be like Einstein counting on his fingers. Why on earth would he have had a weapon in his suitcase? Of course, Pratt hadn't been killed by a gun, but that might only mean that Abramson changed tactics at the last moment. Maybe Abramson had already killed Pratt before Mrs. Pratt came, and she had discovered the murder but for some reason didn't report it.

Oh, hell. Maybe President Kennedy was assassinated by Joe DiMaggio for messing with Marilyn. How do I know who killed Pratt? And why, really, when you come down to it, should I care? He's dead. I'm sorry. But I'm going to be dead myself sooner or later, with no guarantee of later. Shouldn't I spend more time contemplating that fact and less time worrying about someone else's death? I mean, we all come blasting into this world like a kid flying out of a water slide, skip a few times on the surface of the water, and then under we go. Hello, watch out, goodbye! Arriving, going, gone. We invent notions of the afterlife or reincarnation in hopes that this isn't the only station on the track. But who can believe it? God knows I used to believe it. I want to believe it. I am ready to take a leap or two to believe it. But I just can't. Not now. Not in the world I live in. I mean, I want to believe that using the right deodorant will make me sexy, too, but the evidence is slim.

Mark's voice calls me out of a bewildered reverie as I stare at Abramson's name on the pad of paper.

"Jon. Would you like to see the room where Pratt was murdered?"

I immediately want to say no, but I can't think of a good reason to, so I switch to another favorite word.

"Why?"

"Well, you're investigating the murder aren't you? Isn't it traditional to visit the scene of the crime?"

"I told you. That kind of thing is for the police."

Maria flinches.

"Hey, Jon. We're only an elevator ride away. What are you afraid of?"

My shadow. Guns. Alarm clocks. Expectations. Deadlines. Helicopters. Heights. Depths. Women with goals. Shots. Dentists. Rodents. The unknown. The known. Rubber bands. Icy sidewalks. Turtlenecks. Does he really want to know everything I'm afraid of? The only thing that scares me more than yin is yang. If fear were a pimple, I'd be Vesuvius.

"I'm not afraid of anything. There's just no point in looking at a hotel room door that looks like every other hotel room door in the Western world."

"No, I mean go in. After you called, I got a key from Enrique. They haven't booked it since the murder. The cops say they may need to go over it again if something new comes up. It's just like it was the night Pratt was killed. Let's take a look."

My stomach is starting to hurt again, but I've never been any good at rowing against a tide. Mark leads me to the elevators.

"It's on the fourteenth floor. That's really the thirteenth floor, you know. They skip from twelve to fourteen when they number hotel floors. Can you imagine that? We put guys on the moon but still cater to people who believe in unlucky numbers."

I can imagine it.

"What do you think Pratt would have made out of that?"

I am getting sick of Mark's voice. I want very badly for him to shut up. I'm not feeling well at all. I want everything to go away.

playing detective not all that much fun eh colonel mustard in the library with the lead pipe

The doors of the elevator open at one end of an endless hallway. It looks to me like death row, a long block of matching cell doors. My feet refuse all orders, but Mark nudges me out from behind.

"It's just down here, room 1413."

The back of my neck begins to prickle.

hows it going miss marple youre getting yourself in too deep way too deep theres something waiting for you in that room you wont like you wont like it one bit stay away sucker stay away get away get away flee before its too late

"1425 ... 1423 ... 1421 ..."

Something in me wants to snap Mark's neck. Anything to shut him up. Just a little twist, like the cap off a bottle of Coke. He is really pissing me off. I'm starting to sweat and my stomach is going like a diesel engine.

"1417 ... 1415 ... here we go, 1413. This is going to be cool."

I stand back as he slides the card into the lock, then pushes the door open and stands back. Putting his hand between my shoulder blades, he guides me into the darkened room. I lean back against his hand, resisting but moving further in nonetheless. Mark doesn't turn the lights on. The bed is a bit rumpled but unslept in. A suitcase lies open on a stand, clothes hanging out. I look over to the sliding glass door that opens to the balcony. There, almost blending in with the curtains and the darkness, stands Richard Pratt. The metallic Moby Dick extends from his chest like a bloated golden tick. He is the color of pus, and his empty eyes fix on mine as he lifts his arm and points at me. His mouth is moving, but no sound comes out. Then, from a deep, hidden place comes a guttural whisper, "My secret. You know my secret. You cannot be allowed to tell my secret."

happy now

I back away, starting to gag. I bump into someone—Mark, I'm sure—but I turn and find myself staring into the leering face of Uncle Lester.

"I will kill us all," he says, his Adam's apple moving up and down like a bobber.

secrets secrets everywhere secrets

I stumble out the door and down the hall, leaving a trail of vomit.

TWENTY-THREE

It's piling up now. Pratt's secret, my secret, now hallucinations to join the voices. I've fallen off the wall, but I've got to get Judy back to Good Shepherd before Humpty Dumpty hits the ground. They've given me a check-in date now, but it's still a few weeks away, and a few weeks is light years to a speck of a man like me.

I'm comatose for a few days after the hotel visit. When I have a portion of my wits back, I decide to use the time I have left to finish everything associated with this Pratt business. Then I'll return Judy to—oh, that's right—New Directions, and I'll be free to be my freedom-loving self. Free not as in flying, but as in falling.

I even make a list. It's short. First is to talk a second time to Professor Abramson. I am sure he didn't kill Dr. Pratt, but I need to find out about that gun. Academic conferences are rife with infectious ideas, but they are not physically dangerous places. Why would Abramson, of all people, have been packing heat, as Mickey would say?

For his part, Abramson seems surprisingly content to see me. He has a lighter spirit this time around and appears willing to talk. He asks me how the investigation is going, and I say I am having about as much luck as I had with advanced linguistics.

"The study of words, Mr. Mote, is not to be undertaken lightly. Words are at once the butterflies and nuclear bombs of human intercourse. Delicate, lovely, flitting, but also able, in the same moment, to blow us up and scatter our minds and hearts to the winds."

Sounds like a description of some of my conversations with Zillah.

"I don't believe people in my former profession take words seriously enough any longer. They care about words the way a nineteen-year-old boy cares about sex. Words are a game to them. They can be inflated and deflated like a balloon. They're cotton candy, impressive enough to the eye and sweet to the taste, but ultimately just spun sugar, a wisp of sweetened air."

I don't know if Abramson has Pratt in mind when he says this, but I sure do. I still don't believe Abramson killed him, but if you're looking for motive I can see why he might have wanted to see the last of Pratt. Pratt and everything he represented were the Mongols at the gates of Vienna. He wasn't simply a competitor, he was a barbarian. And Pratt had orchestrated Abramson's hasty departure from the department he had served for decades. I need to find out about that gun.

After a bit of small talk I get to what I came for.

"Professor Abramson, I don't want to take up a lot of your time. I've come today just to ask about one thing."

"Yes."

"You stayed at the hotel the night Dr. Pratt was killed, right?"

"That's correct. I had friends from out of town at that conference, a few old war horses like myself that I wanted to spend time with, and staying overnight at the hotel was the best way to do so."

"I've been told … which is the thing I want to ask you about. I've been told that you, well, had a gun with you that night."

Professor Abramson looks startled, as though I am a suspicious wife holding up a lipstick-smeared handkerchief. He picks up his bust of Bartók and turns it over in his hands, like before. I want to help him out. I want to point out that, of course, Pratt had not been shot, so there is nothing particularly incriminating about having a gun. But I can't get anything out.

He finally speaks.

"Yes, I had a gun … I purchased it at a pawn shop two weeks earlier. I had never touched a gun before in my life. It was heavier than I had expected. But the handle felt good in my hand, and the bullet chamber and barrel were fascinating—cold, precise, sinister, shaped for death. I had never expected holding a gun to be an aesthetic experience. It was like caressing a Duchamp-Villon sculpture in your hands."

Abramson's voice trails off, and I can see he is inspecting the thing in his mind, turning it over and over.

"But, of course, you want to know why I had the gun. Maybe I was planning to kill Dr. Pratt, but when the time came I used a knife instead. Is that it?"

"That's not what I'm saying, but it's something the police would pursue, if they knew about the gun—which they don't."

Abramson looks up from the statue of Bartók and directly at me with deep weariness.

"Let me tell you a story, Mr. Mote."

He pauses briefly.

"The river Danube runs through my hometown. It divides the city into the Buda hills and the plains of Pest—hence, Budapest. You can take cruises in elegant ships that dock along the bank near the Chain Bridge below the Buda Castle, one of the most beautiful urban settings in the world."

Why the tourist information?

"Things have not always been beautiful at this point in the river, however. Near the end of World War II, the pro-Nazi Arrow Cross Party was in charge of the country for a while. They murdered, or deported for murder elsewhere, tens of thousands of people, mostly Jews."

Abramson looks away from me and into the past.

"But big numbers disguise as well as reveal. You know the observation attributed to Stalin regarding one death being a tragedy and a million deaths a statistic."

I don't, but it doesn't matter.

"More helpful than big numbers is to know something about how these people died and who they were—with names and places and times. One of the more creative ways of murdering was to take people to this place along the Danube, between the bridge and the Parliament building, and to make them take their clothes off for later reuse—then shoot them in the head and tip them into the river."

My problems suddenly seem very small.

"Sometimes, to save bullets—and to provide sport—they would rope a number of people together, then shoot the first person in the head and push them all in. The first person would sink, dragging the living ones down into the winter waters."

"That's horrible," I say feebly.

"Yes, horrible." He pauses.

"My father was one of those people. His name was Oskar Abramson, husband of Gretta Abramson, and an engineer. He was murdered March 1, 1945. I was twelve years old."

"I'm very sorry, Professor Abramson."

"I tell you this, Mr. Mote, to let you know that at a very young age I saw with my own eyes people killed for their ideas—as well as for their religion. I do lament much of what Dr. Pratt stood for, and he did make my own life more difficult. But kill him for it? No, I am not on the side of ideological murderers."

He pauses again.

"The gun wasn't for Dr. Pratt. My intention that night was to kill my...'"

My head jerks back involuntarily.

"I'm sixty-six years old, Mr. Mote. I had been at this school thirty-two years. The average ambitious scholar these days stays at a place like this three to five years, just long enough to publish a splashy book or two in order to gain the attention of the next most prestigious institution up the ladder. These people are like baseball free agents. Schools rent them for a time for their mutual benefit, but with no expectation of loyalty or extended service. Some don't get through a new box of paper clips before they move on.

"I, on the other hand, have been here since slightly before the Jurassic period, and I am just as dated. I am nearly extinct. There are very few of us left."

"Us?"

"People who believe in the old triad of the Good, the True, and the Beautiful. And in the ability of reason to help us discover all three. People who believe in the mind and the imagination and the spirit as more than chemical interactions—and who value greatly the creations that result when those things engage the world. People who believe that all these things offer us protection against chaos and meaninglessness and totalitarianism and 'might is right' and, yes, against injustice."

"I see what you mean. Not exactly the prevailing view, is it? But sounds good to me."

"Sounds good to you, Mr. Mote? Then why didn't you stand up for it when you were a student here?"

I decide to take that to be a rhetorical question.

"Now we are told there's no such thing as Truth, Beauty, and Goodness. There's only power. The former are empty of meaning until the latter fills them up in whatever way suits it. Those in power assert whatever truth works best for them. Given that the powerful rule over a self-evidently unjust and corrupt world, the only ethical thing to do, we are told, is to destroy existing notions of truth in the name of the oppressed, thereby undercutting the powerful architects of so-called truth."

I want to get us back to the gun, but I just sit quietly. Abramson speaks with growing intensity.

"And I have to tell you it's more than a little disturbing to have spent a lifetime fighting for justice and human rights and have it suggested that one is a representative of the oppressive patriarchal, racist, homophobic status quo. Very few of our students realized I was *at* the Edmund Pettus Bridge on March 7, 1965. I was there. In Selma. In Alabama. I can point myself out in the newsreel footage. I had my head split open with a club. I was on the front lines when my avant-garde colleagues were still going to high school dances—segregated dances to boot. And then to be politely edged aside with this maddening condescension, this unspoken but unmistakable suggestion that you are tainted, retrograde, a slight embarrassment to the department, the profession, and yourself. It's more than one can bear."

I feel like I should deflect him before he has a stroke—or makes a confession.

"You wouldn't want to talk this way to the police, Professor Abramson. They'd be thinking 'motive' the whole time."

Abramson is a bit chagrined. He sits back for a moment, then speaks calmly again.

"Thank you for the advice. I'm sorry for the tirade. The point I want to make is that the gun was intended for me, not for anyone else. But it wasn't because I lost my place in the department and in the profession, painful as that has been. I'm optimistic enough to think my values may return to the profession someday, once the current crowd has squandered their inheritance.

"It is really something more personal than that. You see, a while back my doctor told me there was a better-than-ever chance that I am in the earliest stages of dementia, perhaps Alzheimer's. He didn't want to say it, but I pressed him. There's a history of it in my family—on both my mother's and father's side. Dementia is not directly genetic, but a propensity runs in families, and I have some early indications that aren't conclusive but also aren't encouraging."

"I'm sorry."

"Yes, I'm sorry too. I am a man who has put all his eggs in one basket. God became irrelevant to me when he failed to show up at the river on March 1, 1945. Since I was fifteen, I have lived exclusively for the life of the mind. That's when I first read Pater. He talked directly to my spirit. We are most intensely alive in the midst of a powerful aesthetic experience. These moments are necessarily transient but they can be pursued and cultivated. They happen most often in the presence of great art and music and literature. I vowed, like Pater, to burn with a gem-like flame for however long I could.

"And I think I've done that, more or less. But I wonder now if it's sufficient. Necessary, yes. But sufficient, I'm not sure. I wonder if I haven't been building castles in the clouds. How many people can do it, for one thing? One percent of the population, two at most? Who can devote a lifetime to reading and thinking and sifting and wondering? Somebody's got to fix lunch and pave the streets. How many even want to?

"And what's it all worth if in the end the brain starts erasing itself? All this learning, all this erudition, all the countless connections between this bit of poetry and that bit of philosophy and that musical phrase. All the personal experience, all the conversations, all the study, all the accomplishments, all the suffering—all leaking away, all falling slowly but inexorably toward zero. And, in my case, reaching that point more quickly than expected.

"That, Mr. Mote, is why I had a gun in my suitcase that night. I thought it an appropriate place to assist nature in what it was doing to me anyway. No loved ones finding the body, no desecration of home—polluting it with ugly memories—no tacky melodrama. Just a rational decision, a corresponding physical action, and a quick end to what must end no matter what one wishes."

"Why didn't you do it?"

"A question I've pondered often since. I think I didn't do it because once I knew I *could* do it, I didn't have to. Does that make any sense?"

It doesn't, quite, but I don't say so.

"I actually had the gun out and loaded. I was sitting on my bed. I even had a suicide note on the floor near the door so the maid could see it before she'd have to see me. And then it occurred to me that since I had made the decision to kill myself, the question of *when* I killed myself was more or less irrelevant.

"It was freeing, really. This was a sovereign decision, not one driven by necessity. I didn't *have* to kill myself, I just had to have the right to do so when I wanted, if I wanted. And at that particular point, I decided I didn't really want to. Still some books to read and music to hear and conversations to have. And I haven't really felt the need to do it since. When I do die, by my own hand or otherwise, it will be all over. No angels taking me home. Just an instant and eternal extinguishing of the spark. I can make it be all over whenever I wish. So why not experience a bit more of life—and art—in the meantime? Do you see?

"Yes. Very reasonable, I must admit."

"So, I simply put the gun back in the suitcase. And I went away from the hotel with a lighter heart than I've had in years, only to hear the news of Dr. Pratt's death. He was a man of good intentions. He didn't deserve that kind of death. And I certainly wasn't the one who killed him."

TWENTY-FOUR

I'm not sure how long it is between completing the first thing on my list—seeing Professor Abramson—and addressing the second, reporting in to Mrs. Pratt. Like I said before, I'm not very good at keeping track of time. Zillah bought me calendars and day planners and cuckoo clocks and clocks with alarms and watches with buzzers and who knows what all. None of it did any good. I would be fine for weeks at a time, but when things started going bad—and they always did eventually—I just got indifferent about the tick tick tick and the "you gotta be there" of everyday life.

Why all this obsession with time anyway? With measuring it, meting it out, cutting it up into little sellable bits, complaining how heavy on the hands it is, then lamenting its passing, whining how little time we have in life but always inventing new ways to kill it. Why can't we be suspended in time like fish in water, breathing it in and out, but not thinking about it, not *doing* anything with it, just floating? Maybe it's the sun. If the sun didn't keep going up and down, day after day, we wouldn't be reminded so much of time and its passing. The sun pushes people out of bed, says "Do something!" then drags them all back to that same bed every night. But if it wasn't the sun it would be the seasons, or the migration of elk, or the thump thump thump of our beating hearts.

Anyway, as I prepare to go see Mrs. Pratt, I notice how trashed the houseboat is again. When I fade away like this, all civilizing instincts go with me. I start living like a cave man, gnawed dinosaur ribs laying around the living room and all that. Only its quick-fried, lab-created orange puffs. I don't know why that is. I don't even like quick-fried, lab-created orange puffs. All I know is that I eat a lot of them when I'm low. This time I find five empty bags stuffed into the sugar canister on the counter. If you're an alcoholic you have an excuse for not remembering things. But five empty bags of orange puffs? How would it have been for Faulkner if he'd woken up with orange fingertips instead of a hangover? They never would have given him the Nobel.

Maybe eating junk food is a form of self-medicating. God knows all the pills I've taken over the years haven't worked. But then, what does it mean to say pills for the mind are *working*? Working to do what? Make me happy? Keep me quiet? Balanced? Balanced between what and what? Is balanced just a nice word for sedated? Dormant?

And then there's the talking cure. Zillah and I talked at each other until we exhausted ourselves and the English language. Then we went to therapists and talked some more. They said things like, "What I hear you saying is …" and I wanted to shout, "What you hear me saying is that my life is all screwed up and I don't see why I'm paying you a thousand dollars an hour to verify it!" Because you see the bottom line—whether arrived at through pills or talking or self-inspection—was that I am a loser, and sometimes a jerk to boot. This was the conclusion Zillah came to on her own, for free, the same one the therapists eventually arrived at after racking up enough hours to pay for their vacation homes.

Zillah said I was messed up, but of course the pros needed more expensive names. Whatever the diagnoses, the end result was release for Zillah and more pills for me. The pills have changed over the years—in color and composition and quantity—but none have soothed the confusion in my heart. I just don't know who to be, or how to be—or, for that matter, why to be.

Maybe Pratt was right. Maybe we're like the card section at a 1950s college football game. At the count of three the cards go up, and I'm a pretty good guy with a reasonable chance for success and happiness. Count to three again, the cards flip, and I'm an over-educated, over-medicated, overwhelmed underachiever leaving a trail of broken relationships and orange-colored crumbs. Count another three and, who knows, maybe the cards come up blank. Flip, you win. Flip, you lose. Flip, your life is over.

This round it's flip, time to talk again with Mrs. Pratt. I don't take Judy with me. Don Quixote is going to have to tilt at this particular windmill without Sancho.

When I sit down in Mrs. Pratt's living room, I don't know whether I am going to thank her and quit, or accuse her of murder.

So of course I talk about Memphis. I don't come right out and say that I didn't learn anything useful for discovering her husband's killer. And for sure I don't tell her what I did in fact learn—that her husband as a young man was involved in a lynching. Instead, I give her a factual, chronological account of what I did (I don't mention Judy) and when and with whom. I tell it like a novelist might—creating the illusion that, at any moment, something meaningful might happen. But in the end the story comes to no climax. It just expires of natural causes, like a lot of lives and novels these days.

Mrs. Pratt accepts the report with equilibrium. She hadn't expected anything from the trip and is not upset when her non-expectations are met. She asks me if I have anything else to report. I tell her about my second meeting with Abramson, but don't mention the gun, because she doesn't know about it and there's no reason she needs to. Not very professional on my part, but I feel a certain loyalty to Abramson, and I'm not, as I've made clear to everyone, a professional anyway.

She is making motions that signal the meeting is over when I offer that there's one more thing. A rather big thing.

"I don't know exactly how to say this, but the most important thing I've discovered has to do with you, Mrs. Pratt."

"With me? How so?

"Well, I was contacted by a woman, who for the time being at least I'd rather not name. She says she saw you at the hotel the night your husband was murdered."

"Why is that important? Even if I were at the hotel, that would hardly be incriminating. I was, after all, his wife—a wife who loved her husband."

"True on both counts, I'm sure. But I'm afraid she also suggested a reason you might ... hypothetically, of course ... you might have had ... well, she suggested a motive you might have had."

"A motive for being at the hotel?"

"More like ... in a manner of speaking ... a motive for ... I should say ... committing murder."

Mrs. Pratt does not seem startled or even offended.

"And what motive would that be?"

"Well, she says that she and Dr. Pratt were ... that is, her claim, and of course it's just her word on it, is that she and Dr. Pratt were ..."

"Lovers?"

"Well, yes, having an affair, I guess. And she said he was planning on divorcing you and marrying her."

I am prepared for any number of responses—anger, denials, tears, stony silence. I'm not ready for laughter. Not a short, sardonic laugh, but a deep-in-the-belly, mouth open, gasping for air kind of laugh. It momentarily erases the tiredness in Mrs. Pratt's face and makes her look a decade younger and even more attractive. After a few moments she winds down.

"I'm sorry for laughing, Mr. Mote. I don't want to be mean. It just struck me, after all I've been through, as ... I don't know, spectacularly funny."

It doesn't seem wise on my part to smile. I've never considered the humor of being accused of murder, so I just raise my eyebrows to indicate that I am prepared to hear more.

"Oh, that poor woman. I know exactly how she feels. You don't have to worry about protecting the identity of my accuser. It was Brianna Jones, no doubt."

"You do know about Brianna Jones, then?"

"Brianna Jones today, Charlotte Jameson before her, Alexis somebody before that. Who knows, maybe Brian Jones tomorrow."

"I see."

"My husband liked women, Mr. Mote. He especially liked young, pliable women, though he really wasn't all that picky. He was a very charming man, as you know. He never believed he was doing anything wrong. He even offered to keep me informed about his affairs, as you call them, if I wished, so there would be no deceit in our relationship. I guess I was modern enough not to impose sexual boundaries—that was his phrase—but old-fashioned enough not to want oral reports.

"It's an interesting word, isn't it, Mr. Mote? Affairs. Nicely neutral and helpfully vague. Like 'affairs of state'—matters to be dealt with, things to be inspected. Nothing objectionable or unpleasant or, heaven forbid, tacky. One could have 'affairs,' tastefully, and still be one of the good people."

Mrs. Pratt is holding court with herself and passing her life in review. She picks up where she left off during our first conversation.

"I told you before about Richard's first wife and first teaching job. I was a graduate student at Memphis State. I took two classes from him and then became his teaching assistant. It was absolutely the best time of my life. I was young, independent, my head filled with ideas and ideals, my heart brimming with commitment to every right cause and ... well ... brimming also with what I took to be love.

"Richard was so damned handsome. I never wanted to admit that was an important part of what attracted me. I was too deep for that. I always said it was his intellectual brilliance and his use of that brilliance in defense of the rights of women and the marginalized. He would just fill up a seminar room with wave after wave of eye-opening analysis and insight. He made you see things that were absolutely shaping your life and yet had been invisible to you. He knocked down whole cultural and intellectual systems in a few paragraphs, leaving you frightened and thrilled. He took apart your favorite novel and showed you how naive you were to like it for the reasons you thought you liked it. Then, offhandedly almost, he did the same for your politics, your religion, your morals, and your favorite flavor of ice cream."

I'd heard this story before, and lived it myself, without the love part.

"I remember the first time he asked me to sleep with him. He was so graceful. He said he realized I would probably think it wrong to sleep with a married man, and that, from a certain point of view, it *was* wrong. But then he said something about how strictures against open love between consenting adults were the afterglow of religious taboos built on the need to control women's bodies and preserve religious and commercial hegemony—or something like that. But he also assured me that he understood if I was wedded to that kind of morality, and certainly wouldn't think less of me if I said no. He actually used the world 'wedded' because I remember that little smile of his when the word came out."

Mrs. Pratt smiles to herself, as if ready to succumb to him even now.

"Needless to say I hopped into the sack as fast as my little liberated feet would carry me. Far be it from me to stand in the way of humanity's progress toward boundaryless freedom."

She pauses again.

"But he was never crass or demeaning. I never had the feeling that we were sneaking or doing anything behind anyone's back. He was never nervous or rushed or distracted. He was thoughtful and kind and, I don't know, charming. That's such a weak word these days, but Richard was charming in the original sense—he put a kind of spell on you.

"Eventually I really did fall in love. I couldn't imagine life without him."

So much for the vaunted power of the imagination.

"But I was finishing my master's thesis and I knew I wasn't going on for a doctorate, though he said I should. Said he could make it pretty easy for me. But, ironically, the more I loved him, the less I loved literature. I mean, once you learn the hermeneutical tricks, it gets old fast.

"Anyway, I knew something had to happen, because I couldn't just hang around after finishing my degree and wait for him to knock on my door. So, I'm sorry to say now, I played the injured mistress: 'If you love me, you'll leave her and marry me!' 'How can you face a lifetime with a woman who can't hope to understand you?' 'Neither one of you is to blame—you were different people when you got married.' But my best one was 'I don't think even God counts marriages out of high school.'"

I wonder if there is a similar loophole to cover Zillah and me.

"But it was really very messy. His cheerleader wife didn't go gently. She made our lives difficult in all kinds of ways. Said she'd been traded in like a used car, and she was right. I hate to think what it would have been like if they'd had children. Richard fought the settlement for a while, but then one day he just quit fighting and said we'd do best to just give her what she wanted and move on."

A picture is worth a thousand words.

"All that hassle made Richard rethink his strategy. He couldn't just get a new wife every time his libido spilled over. All the emotional scenes and recriminations were too draining. So he took the high road. A few years into our marriage, he sat me down and gave me a long talk about old taboos and new paradigms, and I knew right then that we were going to have an avant-garde marriage if we were going to have one at all. Maybe he was right. Maybe this was, somehow, a good thing. At any rate, it was how things were, and I surprised myself with how quickly I got used to it.

"But that's why I had to laugh, Mr. Mote. I knew about Brianna Jones three weeks after they started up. The poor woman thinks she's the only one. She thinks he needed a soul mate and that she was going to be Frieda to his D.H. She believes the two of them were the perfect union of body, soul, and ideology. It's a very erotic-narcotic combination. I know because that's what I thought. And you could say I'm still hooked."

It's an intriguing description. Instead of cigarettes after sex, maybe Pratt and his lover du jour discussed the link between Gaia theory and goddess theology.

"The intellectual fads are different now than when he and I were first together, but it never mattered which way the wind was blowing with Richard. He was a captain who tacked with every breeze. When you're sailing free, every port's your home—and none is."

For the first time tears appear in her eyes, and she looks away. "You have to be careful when you link up with a man who says he doesn't believe in truth—capitalized or otherwise. Pretty soon he won't believe in you either."

She stands up and walks over to one of the abstract paintings and pretends to study it as she talks.

"Brianna Jones didn't lose anything when Richard died. If she was talking marriage to him, he was already looking for the exit. Why should he risk complicating his life? He had a wife who put no strings on him, a career that told him how brilliant he was, and a university that supplied him with a constant flow of young women desperate to be liberated. If he married someone like Brianna he'd have to face the day she wakes up and doesn't want Derrida for breakfast. She might even want kids—and I can tell you for a fact there were no fish in his lake. Nothing is more tiresome than a lapsed disciple, especially if she's staring unhappily at you over a bowl of cereal.

"Besides, she overestimates his commitment to justice and the class-less society. He was a Gandhi in his mind and a William Randolph Hearst in his bones. You see, Richard never had money before he married me. I come from a long line of filthy capitalists. Richard may have taught that capitalism is merely the economic expression of patriarchal logocentrism, but he liked nice things. He grew up poor, as he pointed out when useful, so he didn't have the usual romantic notions of most academics I've met about solidarity with the poor. He used to say to me, 'I've lived on the other side of the tracks, and I ain't goin' back.'

"In short, he never would have married her, any more than he married the half dozen that came before or the half dozen that would have followed."

I break in as gently as possible. All this is interesting to me and to Pratt's biographer, but it is not directly relevant to the possibility that Mrs. Pratt went to the hotel that night and killed her husband. If anything, it adds credibility to Brianna's charge.

"But what about the hotel that night? You were there, weren't you? Brianna Jones wasn't the only one who saw you. The doorman did too—coming and going. Why did you lie to the police about it?"

"Lie? Yes, I guess from one point of view it was a lie. But it wasn't to protect myself. It was, God knows why, to protect him."

"Protect him from what?"

"I don't know, really. To protect his reputation? No, that's not it. Maybe to protect the image of him that I needed to have. Maybe I was protecting myself after all. Maybe I didn't want to admit, after twenty years, that I was married to a goddamned warthog."

A postmodernist warthog nonetheless. The most entertaining kind.

"The irony is that I went to the hotel that night to surprise him. I wasn't wearing anything under my coat except his favorite little silky bedtime number. I was nervous as hell but also excited. I thought I'd find him watching CNN. I had a bottle of wine in my bag. I figured a couple of hours of passion might put a little juice back in our marriage. I went to the front desk and told them I was Mrs. Pratt and asked them to remind me of our room number. I must have turned five different shades of red. I was sure everyone knew what I was up to."

She looks at her fingernails as though trying to avoid looking at her thoughts.

"Anyway, I take the elevator to the fourteenth floor. I remember it was room 1413, I don't know why."

I know what comes next, but don't say anything.

"The elevator door opens and there, coming out of a room, is Brianna Jones. I know whose room. We look at each other. I don't move. I just stand there until the doors close again. I don't do anything. After a moment the elevator moves to another floor. I get off and just stand there until my brain unfreezes. Then I decide I have to talk with Richard about this. It's my fault as much as his, but I have to talk.

"So I get back in the elevator and go back to the fourteenth floor. As I walk to Richard's room, I'm telling myself to be calm. But I'm not calm. I'm trying to think what I'm going to say first, and I'm coming up blank.

"I knock on the door. Silence. And then he says through the door, 'Please, Brianna. I love you, but I really have to be alone tonight.'

"It's like he stabbed me."

Interesting choice of words, all things considered.

"I say, 'All right, Richard. I understand. Sorry.' And I walked away and went home."

She reflects a moment.

"You know, Mr. Mote, that's sort of a plot summary of my life with Richard: all right, I understand, sorry."

Better than Zillah and me. We skipped the first two and went straight to "sorry."

"So you never saw him?"

"No."

"He didn't open the door?"

"No."

"Did he know it was your voice?"

"God only knows."

She has her arms over her stomach.

"I was devastated when I walked out of the hotel, but pretty much reconciled by the time I got home. What grounds did I have for judging Richard? For judging anything? I had said yes to too many things to say no to one more.

"Besides, believe it or not, I still loved him. And I still do love him—warthog or no. He was tender. He would talk to me. He always treated me well when we were together, and he never meant any harm by what he did when we were apart. Maybe he was—I don't know—a little bit hollow. But he didn't deserve to die."

TWENTY-FIVE

I haven't been talking about the catfish. But it's not because it doesn't follow after me everywhere I go. That ugly, oily, spiky head thrashes into my consciousness over and over, day and night, stirring the turbid waters. All is not well and all manner of things is not well.

The catfish is flopping right now as I sit on the sofa on the boat. Judy is across the room from me in a chair, holding some beads on a string and mumbling to herself.

I see the petticoats, hear my name whispered, stare at the hand of Uncle Lester reaching toward me.

Why didn't I do anything? Why didn't I jump on him or bite his hand? Why didn't I tell my aunt? Did I really think he'd kill us all? When did I stop remembering it ever happened? Why did I stop remembering? Did I need not to remember? Did I need to forget so as to stop the voices in my head? Did it work? It's not working now.

I wonder if Judy remembers. Can she call back to mind that bedroom at the top of the stairs? Those petticoats? Me coming in the door? Her calling my name? She remembers the names of old Sunday school teachers—surely she remembers this.

Does she blame me? Does she think I could have done something, should have done something? Or is it all lost in the deeper regions of her mind—out of reach and beyond influence? If so, I envy her "special needs." I wish I could be that special—if being so wipes the slate clean. I yearn for tabula rasa.

I have to hold on just a bit longer, until I can get Judy back to safety. I have no future without her, but she has no future with me. It's the one right thing I can do.

it wont be much longer were getting bigger every day

And there's the other dark secret. No less menacing just because it isn't my own. It called my own up from the depths. They are kindred evils. A noose. Petticoats. Smiling men. A bobbing Adam's apple. A blank expression. Lust and hate. What to do with one secret? What to do with the other? Who to tell? Who to protect? And what protection for me, a Pip lost at sea? He jumped from the whaling boat and lost his wits. I feel myself jumping now too, a slow-motion leap from a leaky boat into the Sea of Id. The voices say jump.

jump jump jump

TWENTY-SIX

I float, suspended deep in a bottomless body of water, looking up at the surface far above me. I am in darkness, but see light penetrating the black in shafts that reach toward me yet do not reach me. I see the light but am not in the light. It plays above my head like an Aurora Borealis, now brighter, now dissipating, reaching toward me then fading away. Beneath me is total darkness. I feel it pull me, urging me deeper. Its call is seductive. Not sinister. It offers rest, forgetfulness, oblivion, will-lessness. Despite its call, I feel myself slowly rising toward the light. I am fascinated by the dance of the light in the water, its variousness and flitting energy. I do not so much desire the light as I am curious about it. I do not yearn for it, but I do not want to look away. I am not in control. I am unable to move or in any way hasten my ascent. Neither can I prevent it. Nor do I wish to either hasten or prevent it. As I get closer to the probing curtains of light, I hear a sound, muffled but familiar. It is not so much the sound that is familiar as it is the cadence, a starting and stopping and starting again. It is a sweet sound that warms me, makes me smile. It gives me courage. I want to reach the surface of the water. I am rising more rapidly now, surrounded by the light, the sound growing louder and more distinct. I see a shape hovering over the surface. Its outline is wavy and blurred, refracted by the ripples of the water, but I have seen it before.

I break through the water's surface and my eyes open. And there is Judy, standing by my bed, her eyes closed and her arms stretched out to each side, palms forward, as though she were about to plunge into the water from which I have just arisen.

"Oh, Jesus."

I want to say something to her but cannot speak.

"This is your very good friend Judy. I would like ... would like to talk with you. If you don't mind.

"I am afraid that my very own heart is breaking. It is about my brother ... my brother of mine. You know him, Jesus. His name is Jon."

I want to comfort Judy, to tell her I'm okay, but my head is welded to the pillow.

"Jon is not well. He is broken ... I should say, in two. Jon is not his own self. That is, he is sometimes his own self and, then ... then he is not his own self."

I look down at my hand lying on the blanket and ask it to reach out to Judy and touch her, but it treats me like a stranger and does not move.

"I would like to ask you, Jesus, to make Jon better. He is a good person. He loves you, Jesus. You love Jon. I, my own self, I love Jesus and Jon both ... both together. Please make Jon better. Please help Jon be his own self. A A A ... I should say, amen."

I take a deep breath and it loosens my voice.

"Hello, Judy."

Her eyes pop open as her arms fall to her side. She studies my face intently, wary.

"What are you doing, Judy? What time is it?"

She looks relieved.

"It is time ... I should say, for old sl ... sl ... sleepyhead to be out of bed. That ... that's what time it is, Jon."

TWENTY-SEVEN

If Judy is for you, who can be against you? Sacrilegious to say so, I know, but maybe God will let it pass. He certainly has let a lot worse pass, as far as I can tell. Anyway, I decide I'm done with chasing down rabbit trails. I'll just hunker down and hang in a bit longer until Judy is away and safe. But then I get a call from Verity Jackson. She wants to talk. She tells me it won't take long. I propose meeting in Loring Park again. She says one last thing before hanging up.

"Bring Judy with you."

And so I do. Judy is the happiest she's been in quite a while.

"Verity Jackson is a friend of ours, is she … is she not, Jon?"

I marvel at the "is she not." Straight from *Masterpiece Theatre*.

"She is, Jude. It will be good to see her."

"Yes, good … good to see her indeed."

Judy and Verity Jackson exchange observations about weather and life for a few minutes, then Ms. Jackson explains why she has asked to meet.

"I grew up in the black church, Mr. Mote. We talked a lot about telling our troubles to God. I've told my troubles to God, but God has told me I should tell them to you. At least one part of them."

Great. I hadn't heard from God myself since I was a teenager, but apparently he's still chatting up some folks.

"When we met before, I told you how Dr. and Mrs. Pratt had been kind to me, and that Dr. Pratt had helped me get my teaching job and how I knew him to be a good and kind man."

"Yes, I remember."

"Well, I didn't tell you everything."

"Ah."

"Everything I said was true, but it wasn't what the law would call the whole truth and nothing but the truth."

"Well, I suppose the idea of the whole truth has taken a beating in recent years."

"Not in my part of the world it hasn't. And I guess my walking out of Dr. Pratt's speech was me voting with my feet for something like the old version of the whole truth."

I know she hasn't come to discuss epistemology, so I just keep quiet.

"But I didn't come to talk about that, Mr. Mote. I came to confess."

My heart jumps.

"I know something that I wish I didn't know."

Judy inhales. I look at her sternly. She exhales.

"You were a graduate student, Mr. Mote. You know something about academic politics, and you know how even the most high-minded, principled people can be mean and petty when they feel themselves or their causes are being slighted. They will talk all day long about speaking truth to power, but God help you if you try to speak truth to *their* power."

Yes, the academic activists I have known leaned toward the carnivorous. A strategic memo about a colleague could be as deadly as an assassin's bullet.

"I never have been comfortable with that. So I don't know why I stayed silent when Dr. Smith-Corona came to me with the dirt she had dug up about Dr. Pratt. She said she had been doing some research on a contemporary womanist poet who grew up in the South. In looking into the background of one of her poems, she found something online. She said it showed Dr. Pratt to be a racist—and worse."

It will "out" indeed, with a capital T. Launcelot in *The Merchant of Venice*. It's there in black and white.

"I'm not ideological, Mr. Mote. I teach people how to write short, clear, well-punctuated sentences so they can be more effective at work. I'm not interested in cockfighting and don't have time to save the world. I don't call people racists easily, but I also don't shy away from naming things as they are."

"Why did she come to you with this?"

"She knew I had graduated from the program at the university. We had met briefly a couple of times since at local conferences. She said I was a person of influence—that was the phrase she used, 'a person of influence'—in the black community and the wider academic community. She said she was preparing to confront Dr. Pratt with what she knew and that she was afraid he would try to silence her or even threaten her career. She said if that happened, she needed to have people stand with her for the truth. And she needed to have that in place before she confronted him, because she had seen how ruthless he had been—that was her word—with other people who had stood in his way."

"When did this conversation take place?"

"About a month before his death."

"And why are you telling me? Do you think Dr. Smith-Corona killed Dr. Pratt?"

"Heavens, no. If I thought that, I would have told the police. And that's saying a lot. My people and the police have a history, Mr. Mote. There's no part of me that wants to be talking to the police. That's why I'm telling you instead. If you think the police need to know, then you tell them. And if they need to talk to me, well then, I'll talk to them. But for now I'm just telling you because I should have told you the first time."

Great. Another secret.

"Did Dr. Smith-Corona tell you what exactly she had found that showed that Dr. Pratt was a racist?"

"She offered to, but I said I didn't want to know, not then anyway. I said she should go ahead and talk with Dr. Pratt, and if it went badly, I promised I would be willing to hear from her again, to find out what she knew about Dr. Pratt's past. I would support her then if I thought I should."

"Was she satisfied with that?"

"No, she wasn't satisfied. She said something about sisterhood, but I said that was the best I could do for her at present and so she left."

I tell Ms. Jackson that this is very helpful and I'm glad she has told me. Judy takes this as a sign that "tick a lock" time is over and she can rejoin the flow of conversation. She does so with her usual perspicuity.

"This friend of yours. She … she does not seem like … like a very nice person."

your sister wont think we are very nice either you cant save yourself and you cant save her

TWENTY-EIGHT

I'm running on fumes now. The voices are singing, the brass is blasting—the Wall of Sound they used to call it in the music biz.

river deep mountain high da doo ron ron he the spector we the specters ha ha ha

But it's only three days until Judy is gone and I am determined to go down swinging, so I contact the woman who got the goods on Dr. Pratt.

Dr. Smith-Corona is not a cooperative witness. When I email her requesting a meeting she writes back with a curt, "I have no knowledge of the circumstances of Dr. Pratt's death and do not wish to speak to you. Please do not write again." So, given my lifelong desire to honor women's wishes, I call her instead of writing. It's not what she had in mind.

"Mr. Mote, I thought I made myself clear. I do not wish to have any contact with you, period."

I want to say, "I'm sorry, there's a long line of people who wish that—you'll have to take a number." But instead, I decide to sound ominous.

"I think once you meet with me, Dr. Smith-Corona, you will discover that it is in your self-interest to speak with me."

"How so, Mr. Mote?"

"The police don't know about you—yet."

I congratulate myself on the pause between "you" and "yet."

Now it's her turn to pause. She is silent for a three count and then says quietly, "All right. I'll meet you at four o'clock tomorrow afternoon in the middle of the Stone Arch Bridge. I'll be wearing a red coat."

I'm feeling powerful. "I know what you look like, Dr. Smith-Corona. I'll see you then." Just like the movies.

The Stone Arch Bridge is a beautiful nineteenth-century railroad span across the Mississippi into downtown Minneapolis. It crosses where the old flour mills used to operate at the falls, and it's where—about fifteen hundred years ago now—I proposed to Zillah. Choosing that place to propose was one of the few successful moves I made in an otherwise doomed campaign called courtship and marriage. The Minneapolis skyline, the water throwing itself over the now-engineered falls, the ruins of the old mills, the illuminated Grain Belt sign in the distance upriver. It was the high point of a relationship that had all the promise of Icarus with his wax wings. Take off, soar, plummet.

i wasnt waving i was drowning always much too far out much too far out much too far

I actually do know what Smith-Corona looks like. She was an unknown young Turkette when I was at the U, though I never took a class from her. Now she is on the cusp of becoming a heavy hitter—oft-published, head of caucuses, editor of a new journal (*GynLit Theory and Praxis*)—an up-and-coming force to be reckoned with. Still, I'm glad she's wearing the red coat, because I have a history of misidentifications. Pale and overweight, she has not aged well.

She begins with a threat.

"Do you see that woman standing further down the bridge?"

I look toward where she is pointing and see a young woman in a blue jacket looking toward us.

"She's a friend of mine. She has a cell phone. She knows how to dial 911. I want you to know that."

Ooh. Now I really do feel official. I want to say something witty but nothing comes to mind.

"Why, Mr. Mote, is it in my self-interest to speak with you?"

As I always do when a question stumps me, I act like it's not there.

"Did you and Dr. Pratt get along?"

"Why, Mr. Mote, is it in my self-interest to speak with you?"

"Was there any tension between you?"

She snorts.

"As I thought. There is no reason for this meeting. If I hear from you again, Mr. Mote, you will hear from my attorney. And she can be very unpleasant with people who deserve unpleasantness."

She turns to walk away. So I throw down my trump card.

"I know you were trying to blackmail Dr. Pratt."

She turns back suddenly and studies my face—a touch of fear in her own.

"I know you had some damaging information about him and that you were threatening him with it."

"What information?"

"Let's just say, something from his past. Something that would be devastating for him on every level—personal, professional, and psychic."

Psychic doesn't alliterate with personal and professional, but I still find it satisfying that I came up with three "p" words under pressure.

She doesn't say anything. I know from personal experience that she's going through a rapid series of permutations looking for the most hopeful path out of this maze.

"I think, Dr. Smith-Corona, that the police would be very interested to know that, A, you were at the hotel the night he was murdered, and B, you were in the process of blackmailing him."

"I did nothing illegal."

"So you say. Maybe you can prove you weren't in the hotel when Dr. Pratt actually died. But I do think the police would be interested in talking with you anyway, and I do think it wouldn't be good for your career were the details to come out. Perhaps the police don't need to know. But my client does, and I think it's in your self-interest to tell me more about what I already know anyway."

Of course, I only know a little, but I'm growing confident that I'll soon know a lot more.

"I did nothing illegal. I did nothing unethical. He did something despicable and it was right that he be confronted with it. I merely pointed to the truth and asked him to face it."

"You wanted something from him. Please tell me more about that."

I am doing my best, as usual, to give the impression that I know more than I do.

"I don't know where you have gotten your information, Mr. Mote. Why don't you tell me what you think I wanted."

"Oh, I think I'll let the police tell you what I know and don't know. Let me just add this. I have good reasons for wanting to find out who killed Dr. Pratt. He was once my dissertation director. I heard him give his talk the night he died. I am, you might say, a friend of the family. And I know enough about the last weeks of his life to cause you a lot of trouble. I don't think you killed him, but I think you can tell me things that will help me find out who did. And that's the only thing I care about right now. So it's up to you. Talk to me or talk to the cops—and live with the consequences."

This does not please her. She kneads her fingers while studying my face.

"Fine. I went into his office and told him I wanted him to see to it that I became department chair. I wanted him to resign, saying that he wanted more time for his research, and I wanted him to have me appointed chair. He was very good at making happen whatever he wanted to happen."

"And?"

"I wanted him to steer a large grant to me for my own research."

"And?"

"Why do you keep saying 'and'?"

This is going so well I can't resist.

"And?"

"And I asked him, as his last act as chair, to hire my partner as an adjunct professor. She is very qualified and can teach any of the Women's Studies courses and half of the lit courses and ..."

She stops suddenly, aware that she is telling more than she needs to. I am tempted to try one more "and," but decide against it. I dart in a new direction.

"How did Dr. Pratt respond to these demands?"

She snorts again, with a hint of triumph.

"He laughed at me. He rocked back in his big, phallic office chair, put his hands behind his head, and laughed at me. 'I hired you, Deidre. I brought you in as part of the transformation of this department. I made you. I've noticed you chafing under that of late. Feeling your oats, you might say. That's fine. The son—make that the daughter, in this case—must kill the Oedipal father. I get that. You think I'm getting weak, that my ideology has had its day, that the health of the herd requires a new alpha, and that it's time that the alpha has a hyphenated name.'

"That's when I knew why I hated him. All that talk about repressive structures and metanarratives and justice for the voiceless and the tyranny of the center and on and on. Just blowing smoke. He was nothing more than another bull elephant seal on the beach, a beach master bellowing over his harem through his big fleshy nose."

Her face is hard.

"Then he rocked forward, Mr. Mote, and leaned toward me, still smiling, but now barely containing his rage. And he said, 'But why in the world, Deidre, should I have any interest in doing these things that you are, shall we say, requesting?'"

She looks away from me, over the river toward the falls.

"I replied, 'Does the name Johnnie Roberts mean anything to you?'"

The look on Smith-Corona's face reflects the satisfaction she must have taken from the look on his.

ooh baby baby where did our love go please dont leave me all by myself

TWENTY-NINE

getting bigger every day

The houseboat is a dangerous place now—for Judy and for me. It's where the voices are loudest. It's where I seem most often to go away.

bigger every day

I can take Judy back to New Directions tomorrow afternoon, but what if I don't make it to tomorrow afternoon?

bigger

What if I'm somewhere else, somewhere that makes it impossible for me to get Judy back? The chick in me pecks the shell and will soon be out.

every day

It's a wintry December night—outside and in my soul. I turn on the television, desperate for distraction from my distraction. Judy watches without pleasure or interest, because the only alternative is watching me. I can't make sense of what is being said. They seem to be speaking a strange gobbledygook.

daisy daisy give me your answer dooooo

People on the screen are starting to elongate and grow diaphanous like long, arcing solar flares. I am sick. My stomach is icy daggers and my skin is clammy. I must get outside, cold and dark though it is. I need air. I tell Judy I'm going out for a walk. She says something, but I can't understand what it is. I feel like I'm walking around with my head in a fish bowl—the water distorting my vision, muffling my ears and smothering my breath.

I walk out on the dock, then up the gangplank and out to the parking lot. A thick fog covers the river and the banks. The streetlights make only feeble efforts to beat back the cottony darkness. Battered Christmas decorations on the poles plead "Joy to the World."

I walk along the riverbank to the steps that lead up to the bridge deck. The span starts out confidently then disappears into the fog, perhaps making it safely to the other side, perhaps not. Something tells me to follow it out into the whiteness.

follow us and we will give you rest rest rest rest

I walk and walk, feeling a kind of longing for—what—oblivion? It is starting to snow. Huge, pillowy flakes. I envy them their lazy, effortless descent. Falling softly and softly falling. Out of the blackness above, a brief slide through dim lamppost light, then back into the blackness below. An emblem.

I stop far out on the bridge, in the dark between lampposts, and look into the river. The black waters reflect uncertainly the distant lights of the city. It is as though I am looking at the sky. The difference between up and down dissolves. And the space between here and there. These waters here will in time lap the shores there, where Johnnie Roberts lies, way down upon the Mississippi, far, far away. Time is but the stream I go a-fishing in. I would drink deeper.

drink then do it everyone wins do it for your sister

My head is filling up with noise. It's like the crackle of overlapping voices on a police scanner, none of them quite decipherable. The eternal static of the cosmos. I can't stand it. Nothing is more important than that I make it stop. I must have quiet. I must have peace … no matter the cost. Peace like a river.

But then a sound from across the waters.

At first I think it is the din of a noisy bar somewhere nearby. But I pick up the rhythm of it, the alternating sound and silence, the syncopated measures of urgency and release. I turn from the river and look toward the far bank but don't see anything. Still, I am drawn to the sound and decide to walk in its direction. I walk as a dying man in the desert walks toward a mirage, doggedly, without regard for reason. As the sound gets louder, I realize it is a strange sound indeed—it is the sound of joy.

Then I see the light. It radiates through the dark and snow from a distant building like a pillar of fire. It's as if some crystalline spacecraft from another galaxy has set down among us, pulsing with light and life, yet hidden from the world by the fog. If someone else were standing beside me, would they see it too? Or is it a private vision?

It feels like I am off the bridge and approaching the building in seconds, as though time has been suspended—or impregnated. The vision of crystal gives way to dilapidated board siding and peeling white paint, but the light multiplies. It streams through the open door and windows, penetrating the dark, which cannot overcome it. It's as though I have come across the secret power source of the universe.

The battered sign says, "Riverside Temple of Praise," and then below, "Come All Ye Who Are Heavy Laden." I stand on the sidewalk, blinded by the light and enveloped in the music.

The door is open, defying the winter cold, and I find myself moving toward it, both anxious and afraid to see what is going on inside. I want, Zaccheus-like, to see but not be seen.

The room inside is a large square with a high ceiling and about ten rows of folding chairs arranged in an arc around a stage at the front. On the stage is a large pulpit, and behind the pulpit is a small choir loft filled with swaying figures in gold.

About seventy people sing, clap, shout, and sway from side to side before the stage—but they aren't really present. They are transported, you might say, raised up to some other place where I have never been.

A woman plays a small organ at the edge of the platform. It squeals and snarls and surges. They are singing something about Babylon and captors and deliverance, but the words aren't important. Many of the people aren't even singing the words. They're just riding the breaker of sound. Eyes closed, hands held high, a look of exalted concentration on their faces, they give themselves up to the flow like undersea fans waving on the ocean currents.

No one looks at me as I come in and stand at the back. I find my way to the edge of a back row, but stay standing like everybody else. I don't even think about singing, but I find my body moving. I am simultaneously feeling better and feeling worse.

get out of here

After another minute the organ winds down, not stopping but descending to a steady undertone as a lone voice—speaking yet still singing—rises on the air. Behind the large podium stands a little man, hands raised, eyes closed, looking toward the heavens.

"Brothers and sisters, isn't it good to be in the Lord's house tonight?"

"Amen."

"Isn't it good to be the Lord's child tonight?"

"Amen!"

"Isn't it good, tonight. I say, isn't it good to be the Lord's servant, tonight. Aren't you glad you serve the Lord on this cold winter night?"

"That's right. Yes sir."

"Because don't you know, you got to serve somebody?"

"That's right."

"Don't you know, you got to serve somebody?"

"We know."

"Don't you know that no man and no woman and no child can live just for theirselves?"

"We know!"

"Don't you know that even in America—the home of the in-di-vid-u-al—that nobody, nowhere, nohow, can just live for theirselves. The Bible says you cannot serve two masters."

"Yes it does."

"We know something about serving masters."

"Yes we do."

"You cannot serve two masters."

"That's right.'

"Aren't you glad tonight you serve only one master?"

"Yes!"

"Aren't you glad his name is Jesus?"

"Jesus!"

"Aren't you glad you serve the Lord?"

"Thank you, Lord Jesus!"

get out of here no jesus talk we wont put up with it we wont we wont

The little man breaks into a song: "Jeeesus, Jeeesus, Jeeesus, there's just something about that name."

The congregation joins him on the second line: "Master, Savior, Jesus, like the sunshine after the rain …"

Without a break he moves from singing back to the preaching.

"I have some good news for you tonight."

"All right."

"Yes, I have some wonderful news for you tonight."

"We're listening."

"Are you listening?"

"We're listening!"

"This good news is about a man who was down. Have you ever known a man who was down?"

"We have."

"Have you ever been down yourself?"

"Oh yes."

"This good news is about a man who was down and then was raised up. It's about a man who was broken and then he was healed. It's about a man who was naked and then he was clothed. It's about a man who was crazy and then he was sane. It's about a man who was kicked out and then he was welcomed home."

Shouts and laughter and applause.

"Do you know anybody like this?"

"We do!"

"Then listen to this story and celebrate the good news."

At this the preacher lifts up a Bible that looks bigger than he is and splits it open like a ripe cantaloupe.

"How many of you know that Jesus stilled the waters?"

"We know!"

"How many of you know Jesus calmed the storm?"

"That's right."

"And brother Luke tells us that after Jesus calmed the storm they kept sailing across the Lake of Galilee, and they came to the land of the Gerasenes. Now this was on the opposite side of the lake from where the disciples lived. This was an area where mostly Gentiles lived. How do we know this is a place where the Gentiles live?"

"Well?"

"We know because brother Luke tells us there's a big herd of pigs there. And you and I know that Jews do not like barbecue."

"No sir."

"No sir, indeed. Jews do not like barbecue. A good Jew would eat a cockroach before eating barbecue. Because the pig does not chew the cud. The pig is unclean in the eyes of the Jew."

"Okay."

"So Jesus and his homies are visiting the Gentiles."

Laughter runs through the audience.

"Kind of slumming you might say. But there are more than just pigs in this story. There is a crazy man."

"Oh my."

"A wild man. A man who lives among the tombs. A man who lives with the dead."

"Oh Lord!"

no more we warned you no more uncle talk

"Don't you know this was a frightful man. He was naked. He was covered in mud. His hair stood on end ... like that boxing brother we all know. And let me ask you, was he strong?"

"He was strong."

"Was he strong?"

"He was strong!"

"This man was so strong that they couldn't tie him with chains!"

"Chains couldn't do it!"

"He was so strong that they couldn't bind him with shackles!"

"No!"

He broke their chains. He broke their shackles. Don't you know these people were afraid of this man?"

"They were afraid!"

"Don't you know they used this man to scare their children into being good! Didn't they say that bad little boys and girls had to go live with ol' crazy man, ol' tombstone man? And didn't they scare their own selves as much as they scared the little children?"

"Yes, they did!"

"And what was scariest of all?"

"Well?"

"What was scariest of all? This man wasn't just crazy the way you and I are crazy. This man wasn't just insane the way any brother or sister can lose their minds for a spell. Don't you know this man was possessed by demons."

"Have mercy."

"This man was inhabited by the forces of darkness."

"Lord, help us."

"He *belonged* to them demons. They owned this man—lock, stock, and barrel. When they said run, he ran. When they said howl, he howled. When they said cut yourself, he cut himself."

"Lord, have mercy."

I find myself gagging. I feel like I am going to throw up. I tell myself to head for the door but I can't move.

"Don't you know there's a lot of folk today don't like this demon talk. We are too smart for that today. We've done come too far to believe in no demons. The smart people, they say this man is, are you ready for this—psychotic."

"Uh-huh."

"They say he got a disintegrated personality."

"It's busted all right."

"They say he got an identity crisis. Well, I don't think they going out on no limb there. They say he suffers from low self-esteem. He apparently doesn't think as highly of himself as he ought."

"Well, let 'em talk."

"But you know, I don't care what you call this man's problems. I don't care if you say he's got demons or he's got psychological problems or he's got the blues. The point is the brother is deeply messed up and he needs help."

"That's right."

"Call it whatever you want, this brother isn't making it and he needs help. He needs a visit from the one who made him."

"Yes."

"He needs a visit from the Great Physician."

"Oh yes!"

"He needs an appointment with his Creator."

"Thank you, Jesus!"

"So this is the man that greeted Jesus. When the boat landed, this man—naked, filthy, crazy—came running up to Jesus. And what did he do? Did he jump on Jesus?

"No sir."

"Did he say, 'I am Beelzebub, Prince of Darkness, prepare for your destruction'?"

"Oh, no."

"Brother Luke says he fell down before him and shouted 'What have you to do with me, Jesus, Son of the Most High God?'"

"That's right."

"Don't you know that even the demons know who Jesus is?"

"Praise the Lord!"

"Don't you know that even the demons must acknowledge who's in charge here?"

"We know!"

get out of here now if you know whats good for you now now now

"And what does this demon say? This demon begs, that's right, begs the Son of God, 'Do not torment me.'"

I take a step toward the door, but my legs give out under me and I collapse into a chair.

"Now there's many people today who don't believe in Jesus. There's many that don't want to hear about no Jesus. Jesus makes them nervous. Jesus calls them to be holy, and they are naked and dirty like this poor man."

"That's right."

"They prefer their own kind. They prefer their own mud holes down among the tombs. They say the same thing to Jesus that this man says, 'What have you to do with me?'"

"So they say."

"But don't you know the demons know who Jesus is!"

"They know!"

"The demons know who Jesus is, and they tremble!"

"Praise the Lord!"

go back to the bridge theres peace on the bridge peace in the river

"And this ol' demon, he goes down in front of Jesus, like every low thing does to every high thing, and he begs Jesus. I say he *begs* Jesus not to throw him … where?"

"Well?"

"Not to throw him in the briar patch?"

"No sir!"

"Not to throw him in the poor house?"

"No sir!"

"He begs Jesus not to throw him into the abyss. Into the place of utter darkness. Into the place where every evil and foul and God-denying thing is going to be thrown at the end of time. And, oh mighty God, don't we beg the same thing from Jesus?"

"Amen!"

"Save us Jesus from being cast into utter darkness. Save us Jesus from that place where the light of grace don't ever shine, where the light of mercy don't ever come, where the light of love don't ever pierce through the darkness. And don't you know you don't have to die to find such places."

"We know it."

The preacher is in the throes. His eyes are closed and he is bouncing on the balls of his feet and his voice has taken on a new quality, a shout and a plea and a command.

"You don't have to die to be in darkness. You don't have to die to be in torment. You don't have to die to be separated from God. Brothers and sisters, don't you know you don't have to die to be in hell!"

My stomach is pushing up through my throat and into my mouth. I am cold and sweaty. I feel myself fading away.

"And then Jesus asks the man a question."

"Uh huh."

"Jesus is forever asking people questions."

"Yes, he is."

"He asks things like, 'Who do you say that I am?' He asks, 'Why do you call me Lord, Lord and do not do what I command?'"

"That's right."

"And here he asks another question. He asks the man, 'What is your name?'"

A sharp spasm shoots through my body. I want to scream out, but my jaws are snapped shut and I can't move them.

"The man answers, 'My name is Legion.'"

i see the petticoats i see the look of terror on her face i hear her call my name i see him swinging his head around toward me i see his mouth moving and his adams apple going up and down and i cant hear anything but i can see what his lips are saying and theyre saying i will kill us all i will kill her and then I will kill you and then ill kill myself i will kill us all

"What kind of name is that—Legion. That isn't a name, that's a statistic."

i see the finger pointing at me in a dark hotel room i see the mouth moving you know my secret you know i see the photograph and it isnt dickie pratt in the photo its me im standing between the two smiling men im the empty one ready to be filled

"This demon is speaking for his companions. There were six thousand men in a legion of Roman soldiers. The Roman legions ruled the world. A legion of demons ruled the life of this poor brother among the tombs."

i need to get back to the bridge i need rest i need to be free i will baptize myself in the waters and be free

And then a hand on my shoulder. Then it moves to my head. And then a second hand on my head.

"Dear Je … I should say, Jesus. This is your friend Judy. I am asking you to help my brother of mine, Jon."

She's followed me. Like a hound of heaven. Like a goddamned hound dog.

we wont allow this we will kill us all

"You know, Jesus, that my Jon is not well. So I am saying to you, my friend, would you please make him better? Would you please … I should say, please make him his own self again?"

you cant save him hes gone its us now

"You … you come too, you other Jons. Jesus … I should say, Jesus loves you too. All of you come now."

"Do you feel tonight like you been pulled into six thousand pieces? Do you know what it is to be kicked out, to be rejected, to live among the tombs, to be pushed around inside by cravings and desperations and things that don't ask no leave from you?"

"We been there."

afraid were afraid we dont want to die

"Then I'm here tonight to give you some good news. I'm here to offer you some medicine for what ails you."

"Thank you, Jesus."

"I'm here to say there's a Deliverer come to town. A demon-kicking, dead-raising, sickness-healing, sin-forgiving Savior come to town!"

"Oh yes oh yes oh yes!"

afraid

"And Jesus is his name."

"Jesus!"

"I say Jesus is his name!"

"Jesus! Jesus!"

"I say Immanuel is his name. God With Us is his name. Mighty Counselor, Prince of Peace, Lord of Lords is his name!"

"That's his name!"

"Jesus ... Jesus loves you, Jon. And I love you my own self."

Now everyone is on their feet clapping and dancing and chanting. The organ careens to life with electrifying waves of sound. The preacher backs away from the podium, his arms and face raised to heaven. The shouts and singing that fill the room cover my screams.

THIRTY

I have survived myself. I don't pretend to know what happened. Some truths are better left to salamander giants. I'm sure any self-respecting psychotherapist could give an extended opinion. But I've no interest in analyzing it. I've been down that road. All I know is I went in feeling dark and came out feeling lighter. I felt a kind of melting in me—but I can't say exactly what it was.

Of course, feelings don't necessarily last. I've felt good before for a stretch. But this seems different. Not all the dents have been smoothed out, but as I go to bed it feels quieter inside my head. That's about all I can claim. I don't know if it will last. Maybe a week from now I'll be as bad as ever, or worse. Better or worse, Judy still needs to go back to New Directions. I'm going to see Mrs. Pratt one last time, tell her what I think I know, fill in the rest with what I guess, quit, thank her, and then take Judy where she belongs.

I call Mrs. Pratt the next day and ask if I can come over for a few minutes to tell her something important. On the drive over I try apologizing to Judy.

"You know, Jude. I'd like to say I'm sorry for the way I've been, especially the last few months.

"That … that's okay, Jon."

"No, it isn't okay. I haven't been a very good brother and I need you to forgive me."

Judy looks over at me, not saying anything for a moment. Then she speaks slowly but without faltering.

"You, Jon, are my only brother of mine. I will always love you from the bottom of my very own heart."

She looks at me with great solemnity, like a Supreme Court judge, then breaks into a smile.

"Silly boy."

When we get to Mrs. Pratt's, I ask Judy to wait in the car. She's had to put up with a lot because of me, and I don't want her to hear anything that will stir things further. I want to return her to New Directions in as good a shape as possible.

I am surprisingly calm. Mrs. Pratt opens the door to me. I ask if I can come in. Only as we sit down does it fully hit me how disturbing what I am going to tell her will be for her. Normally this awareness would be enough to freeze me. Today it makes me sad but not paralyzed.

"Mrs. Pratt, I want to thank you for the trust you've shown by asking me to look into Dr. Pratt's death. This will be our last meeting. I'm here to tell you what I think happened to your husband and why. I don't have any proof for what I'm about to say, but it is what I think likely happened. I will leave it to you to decide what to do with this information, if it even rises to the level of information."

I feel myself fleeing toward the usual escape routes, and stop myself. Be plain, be direct.

"I need to start with something I found out during my trip to Memphis but didn't reveal to you last time we talked."

I tell her, in as few words as I can, about Dickie Pratt and Johnnie Roberts. I mention the article in the paper after the lynching, and I make sure to refer to the photograph, the photograph most of all. Mrs. Pratt is clearly upset, but maintains her composure.

"Well, that explains why Richard was so prickly about any questions about his past or his first marriage, or anything southern for that matter."

She thinks for a bit longer.

"And maybe why he was so insistent on helping African American students. Not just people of color, as they say, but African Americans specifically."

I haven't mentioned Verity Jackson in any of this and don't intend to.

"My God, I can hardly believe it. You say there was a photograph. Did you actually see the photograph yourself?"

"I did."

"And was Richard himself in it?"

"He was."

"Are you sure it was Richard?"

"I am. More importantly, his first wife was sure."

"Oh my God."

Just an expression of course. What does God have to do with it? Ultimately everything, I guess. Like that snippy sign in gift shops, "You break it, you bought it." Maybe we should hang a sign out for God: "You made it, you fix it."

Then something occurs to her.

"But what does this have to do with his murder? Are you thinking someone from his past killed Richard?"

"No, ma'am."

There's that "ma'am" again.

"Do you know a Dr. Smith-Corona in the English department?"

"Of course. I know most of the faculty. And Richard mentioned her more than once. Seems like they were rivals of some sort. He found her irritating."

That's one word for it.

"Just like other people found him irritating, I suppose."

I explain to her that Smith-Corona had discovered the lynching and the photograph while researching a certain writer. Mrs. Pratt flinches at the word "lynching," but still doesn't quite understand what I'm suggesting.

"She was blackmailing your husband, Mrs. Pratt."

"Blackmailing? But blackmail doesn't kill you. Blackmail doesn't put a hole in your heart."

It was time to tell all.

"No, but blackmail can throw you off a balcony, if you let it."

"What does that mean?"

"I'm sorry. What I mean is that Dr. Smith-Corona wasn't threatening just Dr. Pratt's career, but his entire sense of himself. He had spent his whole adult life trying to recreate himself, to recapture the belief that he was a good man. It was powerfully attractive to pursue a way of seeing the world that considered truth something created rather than something discovered. If one can sever the link between words and truth and all that goes with it, then nothing is what it seems, and all assertions are mere local expressions of a point of view. And then maybe certain things didn't happen, or they don't mean what they appear to mean. We can make ourselves new every day, and make the past new, too."

I'm getting carried away.

"What does any of that have to do with my husband's murder?"

"There was no murder, Mrs. Pratt. Your husband, I believe, made a rational decision. He knew that the story Dr. Smith-Corona dug up was the end of him on many levels. He knew that if it existed on the Internet, it was immortal. That information will be there forever, and that photograph. Even if he agreed to all of Smith-Corona's demands, and even if she herself went away, there would always be someone else who could happen upon that photograph, always a knock on his door, always someone else who might ask, 'Does the name Johnnie Roberts mean anything to you?'

"I think Dr. Pratt realized this, explored every possible way of escape for a few weeks, then made a decision. He knew his speech that night was going to be his last. He decided to stay at the hotel, not for any reason he may have told you, but because he wanted to end his life in a way that would be least upsetting to you. Nothing ugly for you to discover."

I'm thinking, Richard Pratt killed Dickie Pratt years ago, and now Dickie has returned the favor.

Mrs. Pratt begins to cry softly.

"He tried to stab himself in the heart, but that proved harder than he thought. He wounded himself, though not enough to kill himself. And so he jumped from the balcony."

I half expect Mrs. Pratt to start screaming and call me a liar. Instead, she stops crying, composes herself, and then speaks quietly.

"I want to thank you, Jon, for trying to help me. I know you respected Richard as much as I loved him. I'm sorry things didn't work out, and I hope you're able to get help. Please send me a final invoice."

She stands up. I ask her if she wants me to stay until she can call a friend over. She says no, she will be fine. She has become very formal. She gestures toward the door.

I can't tell her what I'm thinking. No, I do not respect Richard Pratt—or Dickie Pratt either, for that matter. But I know I'm like him. I, too, am trying to be a new man. I am not good. I am not well. Which of us is?

"Please give my best to your sister, Jon." She opens the door and I pass through.

"I will. And I hope I haven't done any harm here."

She looks me in the eyes with infinite sorrow.

"There's no more harm to be done than was already done long ago."

Going down the walk to the street, I see Judy smiling at me from the car, and I smile back. Two daft ones indeed we are. But not a bad team for all that.

Judy studies me as I put the keys in the ignition.

"Well, my ... my brother of mine. Is it ... I should say, is it time for another road trip?"

"I think it is, Jude—my sister of mine. I think it's time we hit the road."

As the car pulls out from the curb, Judy begins singing.

"Rolled away, rolled away, rolled away ..."

She circles her little fists around each other like she is fighting for our lives.

THIRTY-ONE

It's too soon to make any generalizations. I feel much better today than yesterday, but there's always tomorrow. Really, how much can change in a single night, no matter how extraordinary? I'm feeling scientific today, and so I decide to let this little experiment play out a while longer before publishing any findings.

After speaking with Mrs. Pratt in the early afternoon, Judy and I head west. Not far, actually. New Directions is in Wayzata, a western suburb of Minneapolis, known mostly for its big lake. It's where the town people went in the nineteenth century to relax, though of course the Dakota had been there long before them.

It's only a thirty-minute drive from Mrs. Pratt's house on Summit Avenue, but that's enough time for me to take stock. I try to think more about the present and future than the past. It's right that Judy is going back. It's where her friends are—even a boyfriend, apparently. She will get professional care—even if the professionalization of doing good is a dodgy proposition. I will be busy with all the things related to finalizing my divorce with Zillah. I am now officially unemployed once more, with no ships on the horizon. Maybe in the future, if my prospects improve, Judy and I can think about being together again, but for now this is clearly the best course of action.

We pull into the New Directions compound, just off highway 394. The place is still in transition—physically as well as in *Weltanschauung* (look it up). When the nuns ran the place there was a very large central wooden building, with brick additions coming off it in two directions, one housing the young boys and one the young girls. Then there was a small apartment building nearby from the 1960s for young adults, and across the lawn the place Judy lived, formerly a two-story, single-family home, for the older adults.

The New Directions people, with money from the government, had immediately razed the big wooden building and replaced it with brick. The home where Judy lived was slated for demolition soon enough, but was waiting for funding and an environmental impact study of its replacement. Might be months, might be years.

Judy has a smile on her face the whole time I am filling out paperwork in the main office. It's like she's back home from a military tour of duty. She's been out fighting the bad guys, but now she's back to civilian life for a spell. While we're waiting for an "entry interview" with the program director, I notice something on a bulletin board. "Resident Assistant Position Available—Part-Time."

The interview with the program director is a bit stiff. She knows Judy, of course, and is friendly with her in a professional kind of way, as one is friendly with a client more than as one is friendly with a friend. We confirm that she has no income or source of economic support, least of all me, but the woman assures me that this is not a problem and that Judy will be covered by multiple government programs. She rattles off three or four acronyms and title this and title that, and I just nod. Thank God for Government.

The woman calls Judy's group home—that's the nun's term, now a "care facility"—to tell them we're coming over. She offers to walk us there, but Judy assures her she knows the way—only fifty yards away, in fact.

"It is where … it is where I live my own self."

So Judy and I walk, hand in hand, down the yellow brick road to the city of Oz. I'm feeling tired, but otherwise fine. Judy laughs and points to the house as we get near.

"There … there are my friends of mine."

I look in the picture window and see a lineup of smiling faces. Four faces in all, on an assortment of body sizes and shapes.

Judy points toward each one in order.

"That's Jimmy, that's Bonita, that's J.P., and that's Ralph—he … he's my boyfriend."

They're waving at Judy and she waves back.

I wave too. It feels like they are greeting me as well. And it's the best welcome I've had in the longest time.

CPSIA information can be obtained at www.ICGtesting.com
Printed in the USA
BVOW02*1946150116

432935BV00002B/9/P